WE SHALL NOT ALL SLEEP

WE SHALL NOT ALL SLEEP

A NOVEL

Estep Nagy

B L O O M S B U R Y

NEW YORK · LONDON · OXFORD · NEW DELHI · SYDNEY

Nagy

Bloomsbury USA
An imprint of Bloomsbury Publishing Plc

1385 Broadway   50 Bedford Square
New York   London
NY 10018   WC1B 3DP
USA   UK

www.bloomsbury.com

BLOOMSBURY and the Diana logo are trademarks of Bloomsbury Publishing Plc

First published 2017

© Estep Nagy, 2017

Map by Jesse Kling

ISBN: HB: 978-1-63286-841-1
         ePub: 978-1-63286-843-5

LIBRARY OF CONGRESS CATALOGING-IN-PUBLICATION DATA
Names: Nagy, Estep, author.
Title: We shall not all sleep : a novel / Estep Nagy.
Description: New York : Bloomsbury USA, 2017.
Identifiers: LCCN 2016041999 | ISBN 9781632868411 (hardback)
Subjects: LCSH: Upper class families—Fiction. | WASPs (Persons)—Fiction. |
Intergenerational relations—Fiction. | Domestic fiction. | Maine—Fiction. |
BISAC: FICTION / Coming of Age. | FICTION / Family Life.
Classification: LCC PS3614.A49 W4 2017 | DDC 813/.6—dc23
LC record available at https://lccn.loc.gov/2016041999

2 4 6 8 10 9 7 5 3 1

Typeset by RefineCatch Limited, Bungay, Suffolk
Printed and bound in the U.S.A. by Berryville Graphics Inc., Berryville, Virginia

To find out more about our authors and books visit www.bloomsbury.com.
Here you will find extracts, author interviews, details of forthcoming
events and the option to sign up for our newsletters.

Bloomsbury books may be purchased for business or promotional use.
For information on bulk purchases please contact Macmillan Corporate
and Premium Sales Department at specialmarkets@macmillan.com.

For Caroline

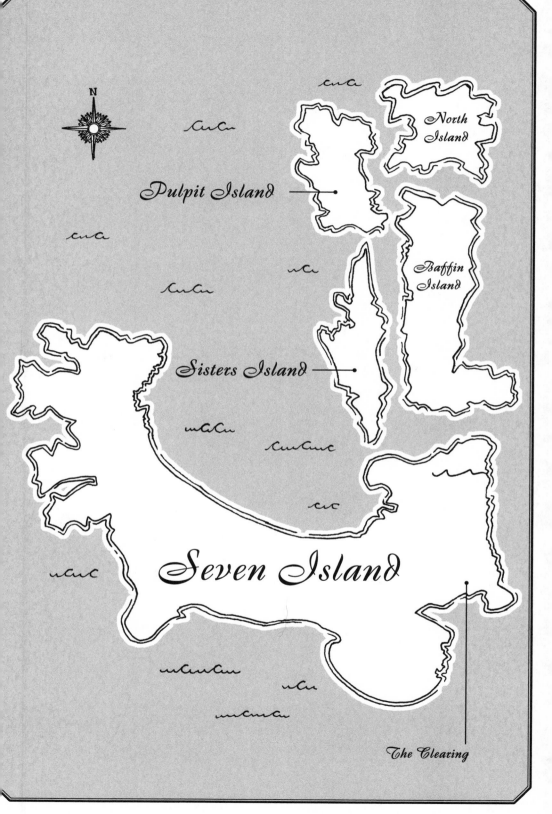

Behold, I tell you a mystery: we shall not all sleep,
but we shall all be changed

1 CORINTHIANS 15:51

JULY 1964

Seven Island, Maine

Seven Island has two houses, one for Hillsingers and one for Quicks.

John Wilkie had heard members of each family use this same odd formula when asked about the island, and it took him a long time to understand why. For many years, Billy Quick had invited him up to Seven every summer, but Maine was a long way from New York, Northern Maine felt doubly so, and with a busy life it was always easier not to go.

That equation had changed during a moment, now fifteen years ago, when he and Billy were for a time trying to repair their damaged friendship. Billy had offered a trip to Seven in a sort of spirit of reconciliation, and obviously to say no in that circumstance would have been cruel. The next day, a letter came from Billy's secretary, asking him to report on a certain date and time to the dock at the end of a road in a remote part of the Maine coast, almost in Canada: he should wait there for Cyrus, the island manager, who would drive a boat called the *Heron*. He absolutely, positively must not be late.

As it happened, Wilkie's flight was delayed and he got lost on the back roads east of Bangor, so it was two hours past his assigned time when he arrived at the dock. A note with his name on it was pinned to the first piling and it said that, due to the tides, the *Heron* could not come back until tomorrow morning, so he should spend the night at the motel in Jennings, which was twenty minutes away.

It was early that next morning, when he was less rushed, when the landscape felt more generous, that he noticed the salt air. Even if Seven Island were to disappoint, Wilkie thought, or if Billy's lyrical memories should prove unreliable, it would still have been worth it to remember how the ocean smells in Maine. When the *Heron* came, Cyrus greeted him formally, and Wilkie's bags were taken on board. He asked which way were they going, and the manager pointed straight ahead, toward a nondescript green portal up on the horizon, and Wilkie was disappointed. He had hoped the approach would have some drama. *Was it possible*, he wondered, *that anything really exceptional could be reached by following a straight line?*

The boat moved out of the harbor into the bay, past a color wheel of lobster buoys, past huge cloud formations, ever deeper, it seemed, into the salt air. Soon the island speck divided, clarified, gained contrast: from nowhere, miles of woods now extended in two directions. He couldn't see where they ended, and it struck him that Seven Island was much bigger than he had imagined. A clearing emerged from the haze, then a dock from the clearing. Two houses, one white and one yellow, sat high up on a grassy hill. Outbuildings and a barn were scattered around, all of them painted that electric red that Wilkie had only ever seen in Maine.

When the *Heron* landed on the Seven dock and the lines were down, Wilkie stepped carefully out of the boat. Majestic cliffs rose up behind him. Birds called. A flock of sheep tumbled down the hill, and the smell of cut grass and smoke ran alongside or underneath the ethereal salt. The sun was hot, and the wind cool. He had never, in all his life, been anywhere so beautiful.

Against his better judgment, he decided that this place was real—and he was instantly and savagely nostalgic. *Someday,* he thought, *you will have to leave this place*. Wilkie was due to stay four nights, but it would never be enough. From the beginning, from that first step onto the dock, Seven Island projected you forward into a barren future without itself, a mainland world, and the only souvenir of the trip was this premonition of your fantastic loss. It would not be insane, Wilkie thought, to wish that you had never come at all.

Through no fault of the island, his reconciliation with Billy had failed. At Princeton they were thought to be inseparable, but their friendship had not survived Billy's marriage, in part because Hannah, Billy's wife, had undergone a political awakening sometime in college, and its real-world effects were all the more violent for being somewhat delayed. Not long after their wedding, Hannah had burned her ships entirely: she decided that their friends, their families, the whole rather lofty world of both her and Billy's childhoods, were all irretrievably corrupt. They moved uptown to Harlem, where Hannah taught in the schools. She stopped speaking to everyone, and Billy let his old world and his old friends drift away. He was not an activist or a revolutionary, that part was certainly all Hannah, but Billy could have showed more spine. It was painful for everyone concerned.

Shortly afterward, as if in compensation, the world sent John Wilkie the Hillsingers. Lila Hillsinger and Hannah Quick were sisters, née Blackwell, and the irony of Billy Quick and Jim Hillsinger marrying into the same family was much discussed at the time. As a rule, the Hillsingers and Quicks each saw themselves as the embodiment of some true Seven spirit and the other family as relative barbarians. They mingled when necessary or appropriate, but rarely with any warmth. For his part, Wilkie grew up knowing quite a lot about Lila and Hannah Blackwell, although without knowing either especially well.

The Blackwell sisters were famous in the small way that beauty sometimes makes girls famous at that age, and it had been more or less obligatory for everyone he knew to be in love with at least one of them at some point. After she married, Lila had sought Wilkie out to talk about her sister, since he was seen as an authority on Billy's character. Wilkie had met and liked Jim, and had often stayed at the Hillsingers' on his frequent trips to Washington. Hannah's untimely death had drawn them even closer, and it was at the Hillsingers' invitation that Wilkie was now, fifteen years later, once again back on Seven Island. This time there was no trouble with his flight, the directions, or the omnipotent tides. When he walked onto the dock, Cyrus had welcomed him by name.

At dinner that night, Lila had laughed easily and at everything, as if the world existed solely for her entertainment. Somehow the most hilarious of all was that on this trip John Wilkie would stay here with them, at the Hill House, which was only for Hillsingers, rather than at the New House, which was only for Quicks. It was unheard-of, she told him, for anyone to have slept in both houses.

Billy may have sent you as a spy, Lila had said, laughing, *but we know you can be bribed.*

2

It was close to midnight and Cyrus stood just inside the barn door, listening for the staccato cry of a newborn lamb. The barn held many sounds tonight, but not that one: the only real anomalies were two rising and falling human breaths. The first of them would be Sheila's, his niece. He was not surprised that she had fallen asleep; she was fourteen, probably too young to stay up with a ewe in labor, but no one else from the farm staff could be allowed to work an entire night this close to the Migration. He did not know who the second breathing body was, but it was almost certainly a child. Children out of bed were a constant problem.

Leaving his flashlight off, Cyrus walked around the corner and stopped at the rail of the birthing pen. This ewe was delivering well out of season, which was a good predictor of complications. Sheila was sitting against a post, doing a credible impersonation of someone awake. He could tell from the breathing that the other sleeper lay almost directly above him, up in the hayloft.

Cyrus turned his flashlight on, and Sheila woke up.

"I'm not sleeping," she said.

The light roused the other animals—the horses, the Border collie in the box with her litter, the barn cats, and insects—and the wave of shifts and exhalations took some time to settle. Cyrus picked up a broom hanging on the post between two stalls.

"Anything gone bump in the night?" Cyrus said.

"Like how?" Sheila said.

Cyrus rammed the hayloft overhead with the broom handle, and for a few seconds there was total silence. The animals all held their breath. The rhythmic breathing also stopped up above, but there was no thud, or scrambling. That was impressive in a child. *Someone historical*, Cyrus thought, *had said something about the rarity of courage at three o'clock in the morning.*

"No," his niece said, laughing. "Nothing like that."

"On my way down here," Cyrus said in a theatrically loud voice, for the benefit of the unseen presence in the hayloft, "Lila Hillsinger was outside, talking about going down to the Cottage to check on her kids. I told her you were here, so she might well stick her head in."

Whoever it is up there, he thought, *that piece of information should send them running back to bed.*

3

The broom handle struck the hayloft floor six inches from the dreaming head of Catta Hillsinger, Jim and Lila Hillsinger's younger son.

The barn had been dark when Catta climbed up the outside rope to the loft. Sheila had not used her flashlight at all, which made it impossible to see her through the small gap he had found in the loft floor. Instead, Catta had listened for her breathing. With all the other night sounds, it was hard to tell just which was hers and which were the horses' or the pregnant ewe's, but then when Sheila fell asleep it was easier to tell. It was so good, in fact, to lie there, breathing along with the sleeping Sheila, that Catta fell asleep, too.

Cyrus's broom woke him suddenly and he froze, and then he heard Cyrus say that Mrs. Hillsinger—his mother—was headed down to the Cottage, where he and all the other children were meant to be in bed. When the boys played the Indian Game, they posted a lookout to watch for adults, and if any showed, the alarm was passed onward via repeated birdcalls. Catta had not heard those calls tonight, but as he walked back to the rope along the loft's one firm, noncreaking floorboard, he figured it was possible he'd missed them from here inside the barn.

4

John Wilkie stood just down the slope from the Hill House, smoking a cigarette after dinner. The harbor lay beneath him, and the wind tonight was so mild that the water was entirely flat. He had hoped to see cormorants or loons tonight, but out on the water nothing moved. Wilkie tried to capture this particular stillness in his mind, almost as if he were painting it, as a counterweight to the unstillness of his everyday world, but it was impossible. There was too much to see and hear. The fireflies were out, and the night-sounds rose up and fell. He would never remember it all.

When Wilkie returned to the Hill House living room, Jim Hillsinger's father asked him if he had seen anything interesting outside. The Old Man was not obviously playing a trick, and Wilkie, hoping to be bland but not stupid, said he was surprised not to see any birds. He did not mention owls for the simple reason that he had not seen any, or even thought of them. Wilkie also did not mention snow leopards, marzipan, a taxicab, or anything else from the world's vast catalog of unseen things. Apparently, however, the idea that any birds at all were *not* present was anathema here—and his hosts began an argument that seemed to turn, obscurely, on a fantasia delivered by the Old Man on the theme of owls.

"There are in fact no owls on any part of the Seven archipelago," the Old Man said, "and there never have been."

"None that you've seen," Jim Hillsinger said to his father.

"Not even owl feathers, Wilkie, have ever been found here," the Old Man said.

"As far as you know," Jim said.

"Cyrus confirms this."

"He knows you want it to be true."

"Wilkie, what I am telling you is not controversial."

John Wilkie nodded and tried to catch Lila's eye, but her back was turned.

"Nothing is controversial when you make it up," Jim said.

The Old Man lifted his vacant martini to the light. "Where have all the olives gone?"

"The owls eat them," Jim said.

"Owls have enormously sharp vision," the Old Man continued, unperturbed. "Especially at night—for movement rather than detail—and as you would expect they instinctively prefer freshwater in motion, which means rivers or, in limited cases, strongly flowing springs. Here on Seven we have no rivers, only shallow creeks, and all of our known springs run underground to feed the ponds, which—and this may shock you—are in fact not stagnant, but rather circulate in *geological* time, so slowly as to be imperceptible from the air. So the owl in transit assumes all water here is inhospitable, and he moves on."

"What we know for sure," Jim Hillsinger said, "is that most owls are built for shorter flights than getting here from the mainland."

Wilkie smiled his precise, professional smile, perfectly calibrated to agree to everything and commit to nothing, and then he volunteered to go in search of olives. A short exit would allow him to see more of the Hill House, about which he had heard so much. He was particularly curious about the kitchen here, which Billy Quick used to describe as *antediluvian*.

Wilkie had been told that the Hillsingers had built the first permanent house on the island not long after the Revolution, and that some part of that structure remained in the present Hill House like a vestigial tailbone. It had been purely utilitarian and had been called the Farm House, for obvious reasons: tenant farmers lived there, and inch by inch they had cleared what land they needed for basic subsistence. While Seven Island was owned jointly by the two families from the very beginning, it was at first only the Hillsingers who braved the mosquitoes and the mud to enjoy the summer days. When they came they slept in the upper rooms of the house, as if they were honored guests— which they were. After the Civil War, the Quicks had invoked their dormant rights and cut away still more forest, hired an architect from Boston, and there on the other side of the clearing they built the New House. Its legitimate grandeur suddenly made the Hillsingers seem like second-class citizens—or, worse, the help—on an island which they had, by their own lights, created. And so began the great modernization. The Farm House was rethought and massively expanded, separate quarters were built for the actual farmers and other staff, and, at least according to Billy, the Hillsingers of the late-nineteenth century began unilaterally referring to their growing home as the Mansion House. That name, however, was so arch that even they did not use it for long, and over time brevity and utility won out and their house was uniformly called, simply, the Hill House.

They were both built in the same broad New England vernacular—*Colonial/Pastoral* was what Billy called it—though the New House was taller and squarer, white rather than yellow, and it had a superfluous widow's walk on top that was thought to be bad luck. The New House had been designed rather than accumulated; it had grander volumes and modern furniture; it was renovated constantly and photographed often, but the truth was that its scale implied huge crowds, who never came. It felt eternally unlived-in, like so many of the grand Fifth Avenue living rooms that Wilkie knew from his childhood, all of them dead spaces apart from each one's secret labyrinth of rules and obligations.

By contrast, the Hill House was a pure product of time. Its elegant facade faced the water, though any other angle revealed it as long and disproportionately narrow; it had been added onto in the back so many times and in such a haphazard way that, when seen from either side, it looked like a train built by a blind man. It had low ceilings, a chimney that smoked, old furniture that was endlessly repaired, unreliable ovens and refrigerators, and more candles than any church. More importantly, there was a genius to it, which was somehow separate from its occupants: it spoke.

Wilkie was routinely helpless when someone in New York would ask him to describe Billy Quick's or Jim and Lila's place up in Maine. He could say it was so many thousand acres or that the butter there was orange and the cows stood next to the ocean, but the facts alone were not sufficient. Instead, he would say this: *Seven Island is impossible.* It was not a description anyone ever found helpful except for Lila Hillsinger, who had heard it not from him but a mutual friend. Lila was delighted, and for a time applied it to everything. She had been raised and famously blossomed inside a world centered on Park Avenue and extending some way up and down from Eighty-third Street. Her prestige in that arena was still such that, during a lunch at the Colony Club around that time, she had single-handedly launched a fad whereby everything good was now *impossible*: *your impossible daughter, that impossible scarf, the turtle soup is impossible today.*

As Wilkie crossed the living room to fulfill the destiny of the Old Man's martini, Lila happened to turn toward him, and she smiled. He already knew that the incandescence of Lila's smile was a dangerous thing, but for that brief moment even Wilkie, who knew her so well, found himself believing that his search for olives had made her happiest of all. Jim Hillsinger, a man with minimal illusions about anything, was not only *not* immune to Lila's smile, but Wilkie had heard him admit in public that he had surrendered unconditionally to it, to her, to the hidden order of hidden things that Lila's smile implied.

Hillsinger had first seen Lila Blackwell (as she then was) at a formal party outside of Philadelphia, where neither of them was from or belonged in any meaningful way. Hillsinger had come down from Manhattan on a lark, the last-minute guest of a friend from college. He had seen her right away, Hillsinger had, and at one point he thought that Lila might have smiled in his direction. Later on, he found her briefly alone by the fountain near the tennis courts, and luck or boredom made him brave. They spoke. And that was it. Hillsinger had decided to marry Lila within thirty seconds. He was a man who took his own decisions very seriously, although the miracle of it, some said, was how he'd brought Lila around to his point of view. When he found out that this stunning girl's younger sister was the wife of Billy Quick, it was already too late. Jim and Lila were married six months later.

5

Across the room, Lila Hillsinger heard Wilkie talk about birds, and she decided that his temporary expulsion, if only to find olives for the Old Man, was a fair price to pay. Neither Jim nor his father nor any of them knew anything real, anything *scientific*, about owls or herons or cormorants or any of the other local fauna. But by saying there were no birds on the water tonight, Wilkie had reopened, for the millionth time, the ridiculous debate on who or what was indigenous to Seven Island, and why. She had lost whole evenings to diatribes on egrets' feeding habits, beaver dams, and the aetiology of wisteria. It could be infuriating, although Lila found it hard not to love the Old Man's depth of conviction about the owls.

Meanwhile, her husband's younger sister lay beached on an empty sofa. Diana Hillsinger had slowly stretched more of her body over the empty space, and she was now entirely horizontal, with eyes closed, as if awaiting triage. Everyone else talked over her, and this pantomime of fatigue or rapture was strangling what remained of the evening's energy. Lila felt she ought to do something about it, so she knelt down at the end of the sofa by her sister-in-law's head.

"Darling," Lila whispered, conspiratorially.

"I already know," Diana said.

It was Diana's favorite game—always knowing exactly what Lila was about to say.

"You're so clever," Lila said.

"I wouldn't worry about it."

"Good," Lila said. "Then I won't." She had no idea what Diana was talking about.

"Catta's a survivor," Diana said.

Catta?

Now Lila was trapped. Her basic plan had been to liberate the sofa by indirection, to ask for help carrying something or other out from the kitchen, but if there was some threat to Catta, her younger son, her cherished, then she would have to know.

"I think it's real," Diana said.

The most likely possibilities were either trivial or innocent. Last year, Catta and James, her oldest, had stolen a box of ice-cream sandwiches from the staff freezer—there was a fuss about that. The boys sometimes chased the sheep, who were already skittish. Whatever Diana knew or had seen was almost certainly not serious in itself, but Lila foresaw the danger of this unknown anecdote, whatever it was, becoming part of a defensive gambit with the Old Man. He could be harsh, and Diana would tell him some small tidbit, often fabricated, to deflect his attention. To that, Lila was sympathetic. In certain of his moods, any sign of weakness enraged the Old Man, and it was worse if the outlaw were related to him, no matter how young. At other times, of course, her father-in-law could be the sweetest man alive. For example, every year the sheep went to North Island for eight weeks of summer grazing. There was an agricultural point to the trip—the grass on North was said to be higher in protein—but one year the Old Man had turned the herd's departure into a sort of pageant, solely to amuse James when he was little and so sick that summer. The Old Man had rallied both houses and all the staff to line the course from the pen at the top of the hill down to the dock, where the barge waited. At the word *go* the door to their pen swung open, and the flock ran down the hill at an absolutely frenetic pace, followed by any children big enough not to be trampled by a panicked lamb. It was festive in a small and simple way, and from those beginnings it grew into something they always did on the first weekend in July. It made her smile to think about, and Lila had never seen anyone laugh so hard as little James had that first time the sheep ran by.

"I think we should seem oblivious," Lila said, still not knowing what Diana was talking about, but nevertheless hoping to keep her silent.

"Oh, absolutely—though no one would ever know just by looking at him," Diana said. "To see it you have to really love him like we do."

Not the ice cream or the sheep, then.

"I'm sure it'll pass," Lila said.

"You didn't see him look at her."

Lila's hand leapt up from the sofa as if it were on fire.

It couldn't be a girl.

Catta was still too young for that, Lila thought. He was only twelve—there had been no signs. And anyway, *who?* Someone could possibly be at the Cottage—the children's bunkhouse always held a random assortment of the extended family's offspring and those of the houseguests'.

"Oh, but they're both so young—" Lila said.

"Have you seen her recently? Sheila's not so young anymore," Diana said.

"Sheila!" Lila said. It had just slipped out.

A wave of nausea rolled through Lila's body, down to her fingers. *Not the staff.* There would be an explosion if the Old Man found out.

Suddenly she felt Jim's hand on her shoulder. *Thank God.*

"For Christ's sake, Diana—sit up," he said.

17

Her husband could be caustic with his sister, and Lila tried to moderate him whenever possible, but this time she stood up and stepped away to let the full weight of his justice fall on this woman, relative or not, who would lie down at a dinner party.

"Meat makes me tired," Diana said as she raised herself up in slow stages, like a prolonged triptych of defeat.

"You should graze in the pasture," Jim said.

"A salad would be fine."

"Cyrus says the North Island clover is high in protein."

Now that they'd started, Jim and Diana would go on for a while. Lila wanted to see her children in the flesh; she wanted to see them sleeping. She touched her husband's arm lightly as she turned and moved toward the dining room, which led through swinging doors to the pantry, which gave on to the kitchen, which in turn opened to the lawn. That roundabout path would camouflage her departure better than leaving through the front door.

"Lila!" a muffled voice trailed after her as she left the room.

"Coming," Lila called back.

The kitchen was nominally off-limits to the family before and after meals, but Lila routinely chose to ignore this rule. As she came through the swinging door, Martha and Susan looked up from the tail end of the dishes.

"Martha, the lamb was perfection tonight," Lila said.

"Thank you, Mrs. Hillsinger."

"If anyone asks, I've gone to the garden for mint."

"Susan can get that for you."

"Thank you," Lila said. "I'm halfway there already."

Then she was out the door and into the night.

Lila turned downhill, away from the mint in the kitchen garden, carrying her shoes and walking on the grass next to the dirt road. She was happy to be free from the need to be charming, happy to see the Pleiades and to listen for the bellbuoy.

All children on the island, those from both families as well as any guests, were required to eat and sleep in the Cottage, a somewhat smaller and much less grand structure built for the warehousing of offspring. It sat by the water, against the forest, opposite the immense bulwark and the dock; the exterior was respectable enough, but inside it was a warrenlike arrangement of bunk rooms, bathrooms, and tables. To her mind, this type of separation was a terrible idea, but the tradition was entrenched and not open to debate. The boys especially would stay up all night, passing out on bare floors just to avoid the abject surrender of going to bed. They woke up late and missed meals, or, as happened yesterday, wonderful trips to see the eagles' nest that Edward Peck the boatman had spotted along the shore of Baffin Island. Although the Old Man rarely came downstairs before noon, he was furious if he heard of anyone in any house asleep after eight A.M. *Like thoroughbreds*, he said, *children must run fast to be of any use at all.*

Looking back up the hill at the magnificent windows all lit up, Lila was sure that no one had ever imagined a better place for a house, for two houses, for a farm. For summertime. It made her happy to think that at some point all of this was a vast entropy of forest. She thought of the time, the unrelenting work it had taken even just to clear the timber from one little parcel at the start of it all, so many years ago—who had come, initially, to break the back of the wilderness? He would have stood not far from where she was right now, would have pointed and said *here*—and then swung the ax. That man could never have imagined everything that followed. He could not have foreseen that she, Lila Hillsinger, would be standing here hundreds of years

19

later, barefoot in a summer dress. That first man would have had to hire teams, feed and shelter them, fight off mosquitoes, mill the lumber, survey, dig foundations, raise walls—finally!—and then, when that first house was built, only then would they have brought out the chairs and tables and other furniture, the sheets and pillows, all from the mainland, all brought on barges due to the shallowness of the harbor. And then, only once all of that was in place and the early fear and labor was forgotten or suppressed—only then could the fragile skin of civilization be stretched over it: the silverware and candles, the china sets, the mythologies, the endless bottles of wine. These dinners on Seven, she thought, were the desperate work of generations.

Lila walked slowly and stopped often, her mind floating, in love with the sensation of drift. She passed the small, sad, disused fountain by the water—one of Diana's *grand projects*—and thought for the millionth time about that other night by a fountain, the one in Merion, years ago, when she had first met Jim. She knew that meeting down to the small details, like a poem one has memorized, and she returned to it often, as one does to scenes of early happiness: searching, weighing pauses and inflections, parsing the silence, trying to see if those first thirty seconds of their common life might not contain in embryo or coded form some prophecy, a liberating secret, if only she could understand it in the right way.

He had surprised her. She had not heard what he said at first, not really: some joke, an introduction; she had smiled, as she did, as much in defense as invitation. It had been a moment much like this: Lila separate from a crowd, her time unleashed, standing by the grass tennis courts that smelled like someone's favorite thing about summer. Jim was confident, direct, handsome in the Classical manner like a Roman statue. And then he

20

had another, more haunting quality, one whose impact was both more immediate and more devastating: he was aware of people watching, even when no one was there. It was not that he was disingenuous or somehow performing—in fact the opposite; if anything he was *too* authentic—but rather that his aura, his whole manner, implied an audience. He seemed convinced that every word and gesture would be noted and measured elsewhere, that they *mattered*, that even his actions here tonight—at the Merion Cricket Club, of all places—would have a distinct impact on the welfare of the universe. That, Lila had never seen. So to be chosen by him—and the choosing was understood right away, to his credit Jim was not ambiguous about that—was also for better or worse somewhat like being cheered by a multitude, a sudden and surprising thing that lived on the border between fear and joy.

That night, she had said no to nearly every question he'd asked. She'd lied about the color of her eyes. It was perverse, but somehow it kept her from being overwhelmed. She also refused to give him her phone number, despite finding herself outrageously happy, attracted, thrilled—*fulfilled*, almost, as in the sense of a premonition, as if here before her was the exact man she had been waiting for. Jim found out her number, of course, and soon the train was at full speed. Lila was delighted; her friends were delighted; her mother was delighted. Lila's father knew people who knew Jim's family, and the reports back were glowing, almost reverent. There was talk of destiny.

In the days and weeks that followed, some part of her did hold back; she had reservations, although small ones by any reckoning. The Seven Island connection was almost too close vis-à-vis her sister. Jim would say only, about what he did, that he worked for the government. There was, perhaps, something not entirely warm hidden beneath his wonderful charm. *And yet he was so tall*, she had thought, laughing at herself, and it became a sort of comic mantra, a patchwork over any half-acknowledged sins. As things progressed, Lila began to feel an unfamiliar sense of surrender, as if decisions were being made by forces outside her control. Surely everyone felt that way when they got married.

Off to her right, the pines sat impossibly high up on Indian Head. At the edge of the Seven harbor, the graceful curve of the shore rose into a hill and then became cliffs. Behind the cliffs, she knew, lay a long stretch of unbroken forest, and then eventually the gray Atlantic. Some part of the old, aboriginal silence remained in those far reaches of Seven, miles away from the houses, in the parts exposed to the open sea. There was something out there one never felt in cities, a monumental presence—a heartbeat without a heart—matched by an equally spectacular indifference. Lila had walked all the way out there on three occasions, alone, each time a commitment of several hours. Each time she had been afraid.

She stopped by the steps of the Cottage, hoping to hear before she went in one more gong from the harbor bellbuoy, *her* bell-buoy, the one to whom, when she had come here as a newlywed, she had laughingly assigned the keeping of her soul. She leaned forward to listen. The sea was flat; the bell was quiet. A low hum rose up from behind her, and at first she thought it was a stray goose or a trick of the wind, but no—it was something else. There was a faint rhythm of speech, the bare thread of a voice. It came from the Cottage, where all the children should have been asleep. Lila climbed the steps to the porch, and the low sound grew to a whisper. And then she knew whose voice it was.

6

December 1941
Park Avenue, New York City

*It was a cold and snowbound December, just days after war was declared
on Germany, Italy, and Japan. Men and boys had volunteered in waves.
Everything—even the passing of time itself—was now electric. For Lila
Blackwell, all the young men assumed a glow of almost unbearable
poignancy, and even their smallest actions—drinking water from a glass,
or smoking a cigarette—had become picturesque.*

*What Lila, who was seventeen years old, did not expect—what had
seemed impossible even two weeks ago—was that this heightened state
of being would obliterate the Christmas parties. The Halls had started
it on Monday, sending around cards citing "the current circumstances,"
and so began a flood of abdication, everyone now competing to express
their austerity and commitment to the war effort. A monthlong
Christmas mini-season of intoxicating joy, of day gatherings and night
parties, fireplaces, cold walks home to bed, laughter dissolving into snow,
had now been distilled down to one magical night: the Christ Church
performance of the* Messiah *that Friday night. On Christmas Eve.*

*Lila did not cry when she was told that their own party would be
canceled, though she did make a controversial request. For, in the midst
of such upheaval in the world, Lila had engineered a hole in the elbow
of her winter coat. The coat was blue boiled wool with large wooden
toggles on the front, and all the girls had the same one: the mornings on
Park Avenue were a parade of these blue coats. I've never heard of a hole
in the elbow of a Crutchfield's coat, her mother said. How do you*

explain it? Lila tried to look grave and perplexed, but in fact she would have endured any amount of shouting or deprivation to get a new one. Specifically, to get a coat that was not that same joyless shade of blue. The war had caused something in her to wake up.

Her father wanted peace in the house, so he gave Lila a small stack of bills along with clear instructions that under no circumstances could she buy her new coat from Crutchfield's—the store where one bought school clothes, including all fully accredited blue coats. Everyone knew them at Crutchfield's, and there could be no gossip about their purchases, her father said, as people were already frowning on all forms of excess, real and imagined, in the face of this naked foreign aggression.

The day before Christmas Eve, Lila took her sister, Hannah, in a taxi to a dress shop downtown that she had heard about from certain disreputable friends. It was called Amaranth. It was on the second floor above a steak house on University Place, not far from the wasteland of Washington Square Park.

The stairway was dirty and decrepit, which surprised Lila, although she did not share this impression with her sister. Entering the shop, though—one was buzzed in—was like entering a beautiful, vacant fairyland where the only sentient forms of life were flowers. Orchids covered the small handful of available surfaces. A lady sat behind a desk. No clothes were visible.

It's the wrong place, Hannah whispered.

How may I help you? the lady at the desk said.

A winter coat, please, Lila said.

The lady at the desk spoke into an intercom, and soon a long rack emerged from a door, pushed from behind by a tiny woman in a uniform. The rack had nine coats on it. They were nine different colors, and none of them was blue. One of them was fur! Another was white. Lila had not known that winter coats could be white.

The tiny woman handed Hannah the coats, one at a time, and

Hannah handed them to Lila. She tried on all of them, and as she looked at herself in the mirror wearing such different coats, every one was like visiting a new country. Each was better than the last—but what exactly was it that she wanted? Should it be beautiful? Sophisticated? Elegant? Each of these words captured something, but not enough. She wanted the coat to be . . . inevitable. In these difficult times, *Lila thought,* in the face of war, a new winter coat must be better than merely warm or lovely.

Hannah tried on the fur one herself, and they both laughed. The lady behind the desk looked over disapprovingly.

The white one, please, Hannah said to the tiny woman.

I can't wear that, Lila said.

Be brave, Hannah said, and she shut her eyes theatrically.

Lila put it on, one sleeve and then the other, and then she buttoned it up. It had a collar that folded down. It was beautifully, even insightfully cut.

The tiny woman who handed them the coats made a small involuntary sound of appreciation. A sharp intake of breath.

Hannah opened her eyes.

You look like a poem, she said.

I love it, Lila said. She did not try on any more coats.

On the night of the Messiah, *Lila told her mother that she would meet them at the church. Since the parties were all canceled, Lila said, she had to drop off Christmas presents en route. By design, she arrived at the church late, when her mother and father and Hannah were already in their usual pew. She would not give anyone the opportunity to object. She had kept the coat a secret from her mother, and Hannah was sworn to secrecy.*

Lila felt the ripple as she walked down the aisle. And after it died down, she thought, the silence was deeper than before. Hannah said later that several people around them had said, Who was that? It was perfection, although her mother's horror was clear from her permanent stare over the next two hours of wonderful music.

Outside it had begun to snow, and the crowd lingered outside for a long time after the performance, spilling out from the sidewalk onto Park Avenue: laughing, shouting, grasping at one another, stretching out the last moments of the old, known world.

Lila and Hannah stood under a street lamp with their arms entwined while boys in groups crashed into them, over and over again. One railed against the absent Christmas, another offered schnapps from a secret flask, some sang carols. More than one proposed marriage to Lila, and she smiled, to give them hope.

Inevitably, the sisters were separated, and as Lila drifted through the crowd, a boy came up to her and said Merry Christmas. He was alone, and quieter than the rest. His scarf was tied unconventionally. Lila did not recognize him.

I love your coat, the boy said. It reminds me of the mountains.

His name was Billy Quick, he said, and—though born in New York—his family had only recently returned to the States from Austria via Milan and Cairo. They kept being expelled from places, he said. Lila laughed; she did nothing that night but laugh, and as the snow continued to fall she found it easy to imagine that this collision of new energies might easily conjure any number of new things in the world, the least improbable of which might be a handsome stranger who seemed to know what her white coat truly meant. Then he said something that Lila would remember:

Would you introduce me to your sister?

7

Lila pushed open the screen door and then closed it behind her again, gently. In the hallway, a line of sweaters and raincoats hung from hooks. She looked from the shadows into the living room, and saw that she'd been right: Billy Quick sat on a couch, holding a candle in one hand and a large book in the other. Rapt, kneeling boys and girls surrounded him.

Draw down the blind, Jim, whispered my mother, Billy read aloud from the book. *They might come and watch outside.*

He looked up and Lila thought he saw her, but she could not be sure. The children saw only the story.

Billy paused and was now repeating himself, dramatically— *They might come and watch outside.*

"And there they are!" he shouted, pointing at Lila behind them.

The children screamed bloody murder. Some of the boys, pitched forward while they listened, spilled helplessly over as they tried to turn and yell and hide all at the same time. When they saw that it was only Mrs. Hillsinger, just a lady in a white dress holding her shoes, they all exploded in laughter. The boys who had not fallen down launched themselves gleefully on top of the boys who had.

"Enough! That's where we stop tonight," Billy said.

"Noooooo!"

"Off to bed! Right away, or you'll be keelhauled!"

The boys tried lazily to disentangle themselves, while the handful of outnumbered girls unfolded their legs, stood up, and melted away upstairs. Catta emerged from the bottom of the pile, saw his mother, and tried to sneak past her.

"There you are!" Lila said.

He was caught. He stood up straight, like a soldier.

Lila looked for a long time at the different parts of his body, as if she were counting his limbs.

"Why were you out of bed?" she said, finally. It was not what she had wanted to ask him.

Lila could see no clues at all—nothing to confirm or deny Diana's claim that Catta was *in love* with the farmhand Sheila, whatever that would mean at his age. It was not that Lila wanted to stop time or to control him: Catta should be in love a thousand times, if necessary.

But please, she thought, *not yet. Give him another year, another month. Do not take this peace from him just yet.*

"Go to bed," Lila finally said. "Dream of kittens and rabbits."

It was what she always said to him before bed, but Catta never did. He had dreamt once of an eagle that dropped straight down out of the sky, hunting a rabbit. He ran past his mother and up the narrow stairs to the bunk room, and as he lay down, Catta was sorry to be in bed and not on the bare floor of the hayloft, listening for the slow change in Sheila's breathing. He was so tired that he was asleep even before his mother had begun her silent evisceration of Billy Quick.

Downstairs, Catta's brother, James, who was fifteen, was asking Billy for *Treasure Island* so he could read ahead. He was desperate, Lila thought, for some mark of distinction and furious that it was being denied him. While James pleaded, Lila chose to compensate for all the injustice in the world by wrapping her arms around her older son.

"Let me see it for just one second," James said.

"I don't remember exactly how it ends," Billy said to James, starting to laugh. "But I will tell you that, in my experience, things end badly for pirates."

James was humiliated. If he had shown up at the Hill House in the middle of the night, the Old Man would have screamed and thrown him out. And now his uncle was laughing at him.

In fact, Lila knew, Billy was laughing at her sudden embrace of James, who clearly did not want to be touched—laughing at the futility and narcissism of the gesture. But James wouldn't know that. He would take it badly.

"That's enough," Lila said.

It was much too late for any child to be up, even an older child like James. Even worse, James's absurd pleading made her feel somehow less right to be angry with Billy for keeping the children up.

"Go to bed, darling," she said to James. "Set an example."

"Why are *you* here?" James said to her sharply, and he left the room. It was typical of him to give her exactly what she wanted, and also to make her pay too much for it. The remaining boys followed James upstairs, leaving Lila and Billy alone.

"Ann and Barbara are so adorable," Lila said about Billy's daughters—her nieces—when he returned from the kitchen. "They have such tiny knees."

"The boys were having an argument down by the tree line," Billy said. "I thought the book might calm them down."

"I see," she said. "It's lucky that you were there."

Billy and Hannah had married very young. Her sister was only twenty, and a few years afterward, in fact just after Lila's own wedding, her sister cut off the Blackwell family in general, and Lila in particular. It could not be put more simply than that.

Hannah was scathing about their poor father, who worked for a big bank. She flatly accused Lila, who was (Hannah said) the clear favorite in the house, of conspiring with her parents to keep her small and simple and complicit. She used that word over and over again: *complicity*. And it was not only Lila: nearly anyone who had known Hannah growing up was similarly abandoned. The happy couple had moved above Ninety-sixth Street, well into Spanish Harlem, and Hannah taught in the public schools there while, amazingly, Billy continued his Midtown life of a financier. Lila's pleading letters and phone calls went unreturned. She had been enraged and then sad and then optimistic and then resigned, and all of it was futile. And then Hannah had died.

Lila walked outside, where the bellbuoy continued to be silent. This little trip to the Cottage, Lila thought, had been a total catastrophe. She had learned nothing about the Sheila situation, she had infuriated James, and she had abandoned her guests. Her mother would be appalled on every count.

"I thought I heard a ghost this afternoon," Billy said as the Cottage screen door slammed behind him. "And its voice was very much like John Wilkie's."

"Oh—yes," Lila said, laughing. "John is here with us. It was very last-minute—I hope it's not awkward."

"Not at all," Billy said.

He was lying, she knew—but still, they could invite whomever they pleased.

"Jim's taken a job with Keene Wilkie," Lila said.

"Really?" he said.

This was not yet public information, and Billy seemed genuinely surprised.

"Here or there?" Billy said. He meant New York or Washington.

"Here," Lila said.

"The girls will be so pleased."

"Do young boys fall in love?" Lila said, perhaps too suddenly.

Billy laughed.

"Don't laugh," Lila said.

"Not really," Billy said.

"But what if they do?" Lila said.

"Then they do so from a distance," he said, "and wholly without effect."

8

The Old Man had the bellows out. He dropped a roll of birch bark on the coals and added a few twigs, some larger sticks, and then laid two small logs across to make a platform. On top of that he put the shoulder of a large branch, a huge misshapen chunk of wood that was so big that it threatened to tip the whole burning pile out onto the rug.

The Old Man turned, and for a second, Hillsinger saw in the firelight an image of his father as a much younger man.

"Lila would never agree," Hillsinger said.

"That's not an argument," the Old Man said. "Where's Wilkie? He knows."

The bellows made the fire jump, and now the Old Man put it away and sat down.

"Wilkie understands because his father understands," the Old Man continued, "while you, on the other hand, choose blindness. Why is that?"

"You're ranting."

"Instead of clarity and action," the Old Man said, "what we have now is steering committees. It's an extension of the chaos under Kennedy, God rest his soul. His father stole the election in 1960—sit down. Grant it for now; think with me *as if*, if that makes you happier. He felt no legitimacy—Kennedy did—since he was accountable to his father and not the American people. It made him passive. He let the Reds have their orgy in Asia. He tried to substitute the illusion of action in Cuba for real and decisive steps elsewhere. Failure was inevitable. And still, even with all those mistakes, all is not yet lost: there remains a bulwark in Asia, *ein feste burg*. Vietnam is the choke point—the narrow bridge. It is Thermopylae."

"The better comparison," Hillsinger said, "is Napoleon and Moscow."

"They have no winter in Vietnam."

"They *are* the winter. The Viet Minh dug a hundred miles of trenches at Dien Bien Phu."

"More than anything else," the Old Man said, "what I want is for you to come out into the light. You've already been broken once on the wheel of Vietnam. *Sit down*. In this room we speak the truth. They painted you as a quietist and then they pushed you out."

"Who told you that?" Hillsinger said.

"Someone who knows," the Old Man said.

Hillsinger was entertained: this piece of wrong intelligence so proudly displayed by his father—that he had left the CIA over a policy dispute in a region wholly outside his portfolio—was a lie that would have had to come initially from the CIA Director himself. It was an elegant lie, one in the classic style: make a small, forgivable charge—that Hillsinger was a pacifist—to disguise the larger, catastrophic one. Given the circumstances, it could almost be seen as an act of generosity.

"It's nothing to be ashamed of," the Old Man continued. "Something similar happened to Allen Dulles himself. He built the CIA with his own hands, but then he lost his ability to see the future. Vision is not, however, your problem: on the contrary, I believe you see the problem very clearly. Your problem is will. You want to be comfortable. Call me a sentimentalist, but I think of Catta, a wonderful child, affectionate, thoughtful, loves the island, loves the woods; on the other hand, he's too quiet for his age, and he's got a girl's name because his mother took Latin once. Lila runs after him. Diana runs after him. He's a bright boy—he sees all this—but the limitation of his world is exactly the problem. You reject my interpretation of the past. Fine. You reject my interpretation of military tactics. Fine. But let me tell you what's coming—yes, that's right—old men know the future. Sooner than you think, little Catta, charming Catta, will face a savage, remorseless Red wave coming from Europe, from Asia, even from Africa and South America. They will surround us, slowly, and then they will act. The Reds will cut Catta's head off and mount it on the Kremlin gate and it will be your fault. Yours. Because you lack the proper will."

"May you live forever, Dad."

"Ha! I'll have to, because of you and the idiot Democratic party."

9

Lila returned to the living room, and all conversation stopped. She smiled and crossed the room, sat on the arm of her husband's chair, and placed her hand on top of his to form a still life of domestic bliss. In Washington, in the CIA circles, this sort of thing happened all the time.

"James was on edge tonight," she said.

"You were at the Cottage?" Jim said.

"For five seconds."

"It's after midnight," the Old Man said.

"The children were up," Lila said. "Billy was reading them *Treasure Island*."

"Why?" Jim said.

"There was some disagreement; I suppose he thought it would help."

"QED," the Old Man said darkly.

"I wonder if the timing . . ." Wilkie said, or rather he continued, it seemed to Lila, along the thread of a lapsed conversation. Wilkie was good like that; he knew that silence was far deadlier than any speech, although in this particular case he trailed off. She could see that Jim and his father were on the same side of a question, and it obviously concerned her somehow. She did not know what was at stake here—the late-night conversation at the Hill House could range widely—but she was ready for whatever came. She was used to living among warriors.

When they were in Warsaw, certainly, Lila had seen herself as standing on the front line. She was watched everywhere

35

she went by the Polish security services, and then also, as a well-dressed American woman, she was simply conspicuous. She had embraced the minor theater of her role, opting for a sort of diplomatic grand manner, a slightly shorter Grace Kelly come to the Eastern Bloc: chaste, elegant, and disdainful of the enemy. She shopped in the empty markets with their empty shelves, and asked the KGB men following her to light her cigarettes. For a while it was exhilarating that their lives resonated on such a grand scale, and as far as mandates went, chaste and elegant were both relatively easy for her—for both of them. Where she and Jim differed, however, was that only she had broken.

Jim was, it seemed, a sort of prodigy of this work—he could endure more and see farther. His mind and body were not like other people's. If anything, the unending malevolence of the other side had energized him. But he was not alone in a foxhole, and, as far as Lila could tell, one either participated in the foresight and preoccupation demanded by life in enemy territory, as Jim and his colleagues did, or one suffocated, as Lila and so many of the other wives and children did. And then, when they came back to the States, it was worse. There had been bloody betrayals and public hearings, Kim Philby and Joe McCarthy, and then traitors were said to be everywhere. Jim stayed up for hours every night, making notes of each of the day's conversations in case he were accused. The CIA was operating in a state of internal siege.

When Hannah died, Lila felt nothing. She had been under such strain for so long that she had no reserves left whatsoever. Her sister was gone, and her life, as measured by the basic tenor of her days, was exactly the same, as if the enormity of the Soviet threat had strangled her ability to experience anything other than itself. She panicked. She let herself sleep with Billy Quick once, and then again, and then several more times, and she thought of those episodes as isolated attempts to retrieve her own ability to feel. She was discreet. Never in Washington, not on Seven, always with a good alibi. It was, after all, only Billy Quick. Even her breakdown had had an air of responsibility to it.

Just then Billy himself entered the Hill House living room, and everyone turned toward him. No one asked why he was in the wrong house, uninvited, holding a copy of *A Field Guide to Birds*.

"Ah, Billy—you're an honest man," the Old Man said. "Wouldn't you agree—"

"Dad," Jim Hillsinger said.

Hillsinger had silenced the Old Man with just the one syllable. *This is promising*, Wilkie thought. He happened to be looking at Lila when Jim spoke, and that one word had also called her back from some phantasmagoria of her own.

"Billy," Hillsinger said, "I wonder if you can help us decide something."

"Certainly," Billy said. "Hello, John."

"Hello, Billy."

"Do you think, Billy," the Old Man said, declining further silence, "that there is any benefit to be had from spending a night alone out on Baffin Island?"

Oh my God, Lila thought. *Not this again.*

Every year, at least once, the Old Man aired the idea of someone's going to Baffin for the night. He never said who it would be or when they would go, although it was quite clear that it would never be him. These Baffin jags would then decay into wandering lectures on beaver habitat, the velocity of glaciers, or the sad state of the Spanish Left. The Great Lie of the Sino-Soviet split. Lila hoped that there would be less of this sort of thing when they were back in New York, where no one she knew had ever heard of Laos.

"Benefit who?" Billy said.

"Does it matter?" Hillsinger said.

"Absolutely."

"Say a young man," the Old Man said.

"Which young man?"

"Ah," the Old Man said, in a poor imitation of spontaneous thought, "say someone young enough for the experience to be useful, and yet old enough to survive it."

"Say Catta, for example," Jim said.

Lila had not been listening; she was looking at the fire. *Had they said Catta?*

Baffin was the largest of the minor islands in the Seven archipelago. It lay close by, just across a wide channel from Seven, but despite that it was the most forbidding, wild, and neglected part of the chain. Alone among the islands, it had no open spaces, and the trees and undergrowth were said to be too dense for walking. According to Cyrus, it was the only one of the five islands never to be inhabited, that there were no buildings or ruins or shell heaps, no trails and no water. The children and some of the staff said there were ghosts. How so much was known, when apparently no one had ever been past the tree line, was a mystery to her.

In any case, that savage register of theirs, the talk of Baffin and force multipliers and psychological war, should all be saved for phantoms and the learned journals; they could not speak like that about her children, not even theoretically or in jest. Catta was a real boy, who bled when he fell down.

Lila had met Allen Dulles once, when he was still Director of the CIA. It was at a Christmas party, and Mr. Dulles, the great keeper of secrets, had been holding eggnog and a plateful of pink sugar cookies. The image had stayed with her. *Your husband,* Dulles had said, *has remarkable and terrifying patience.* Lila did not know what that meant, really—the Director had said it cheerfully enough—but, to her shame, it had frightened her. It made her think of sleeplessness and ropes, of drifts of snow.

"I think Catta could survive ten nights in the wilderness, or for that matter fifty," Billy said.

"It's a question of education," Hillsinger said.

"What are we teaching?"

"Victory," the Old Man said.

"The owls of Baffin," Billy said, "have no army to speak of."

Wilkie laughed out loud, and the Old Man exhaled pointedly.

"So, Billy," Hillsinger said, almost offhandedly, "would you say we're winning?"

That, Wilkie thought, was a dangerous question. In the somewhat arcane policy circles of Washington and certain parts of New York, the wrong answer to that question would be used to discredit everything a person might say in the future.

"Gah!" the Old Man said, seemingly unable to restrain himself. "Catta knows nothing. We need more men, better men. If we can't find them, then we need to make them ourselves."

Billy just laughed. He turned to the Old Man.

"Would you mind," Billy said, "if I borrow your Audubon for the night? I have unidentified birds nesting in my porch."

"Be my guest."

Lila could not, for the moment, look at either her husband or Billy Quick. She focused all of her attention on the little ceramic owl that sat on the mantelpiece. It was amazingly ugly, with outsized eyes. She had tried several times to throw it away, but Diana Hillsinger harbored a misguided love for it.

"Mr. Hillsinger," she finally said to the Old Man, adopting her most refined persona, her mode of unfeigned supplication. Billy Quick, who had risen to leave, stopped and turned back.

"I'm sure I've heard you say," she continued, "that the gulag is better at manufacturing corpses than soldiers."

"Far better, my dear," the Old Man said. "But we shouldn't confuse the vaccine with the virus."

That was enough. Lila stood up and walked outside.

August 1953
Seven Island, Maine

Once John Wilkie had come to believe that Seven Island was impossible, he set about understanding why it was not. On that first trip fifteen years ago, he had spent a damp afternoon in the New House library with a pile of self-published histories of Seven Island written by family members at different points in time.

Most of them began with Elijah Hillsinger, one of the two quasi-founders of Seven Island. In the late 1760s, before the Revolution—when Maine was still a part of Massachusetts Colony—Hillsinger was a small timber merchant outside of Boston. He had a few rakish years before discovering God and his wife, Amity, at roughly the same time. Luther Shipley, a friend from his pagan days, had suffered gambling losses and needed ready cash, which the now-temperate Hillsinger gave him in return for Shipley's title to timber grants near the small township of Jennings. Closer to Boston, both forests and workers were more expensive, and Hillsinger saw opportunity in the dual land-labor arbitrage.

And then it was 1774—a fateful year. There was broad unrest, and the laws were changing constantly due to the greed and perfidy of the British Crown. Hillsinger struggled; there were bad surprises. For one thing, local shipping costs in Maine turned out to be exorbitant—there were only a few shippers in Jennings, and they charged him tourist rates. Cutting the timber in Maine cost a fraction of what it did in Boston, but then the shipping costs were more than triple his highest estimates. To make matters worse, the

Jennings boats were slow and overladen, which made them easy targets for the British Navy. Many were interdicted. Hillsinger's diaries—quoted but not reproduced—expressed his outrage with the extortionate shipping companies of Jennings, alongside his firm belief in the basic model of logging raw timber in Maine and then transporting it to Newburyport to be finished.

He took on an extraordinary amount of bank debt using Shipley's timber grants as collateral, and found a partner with the maritime experience he lacked. The partner's name was Matthew Quick, a first mate for a transatlantic shipping concern out of New Bedford. Hillsinger asked him what ships he would build if he were building a fleet from scratch, to be based in Jennings, which was on a river, and with the specific object, too, of evading or outrunning the British Navy. Quick's short answer was compelling: smaller and faster than traditional ocean-going ships, with an unconventionally shallow draft. Hillsinger liked what he heard, and under Quick's guidance, they built an initial fleet of three ships that were materially faster than other cargo ships of the time, but with much smaller payloads and a draft so shallow that navigation proved difficult for those seamen trained on the larger vessels. These new ships were much harder to control in windy conditions, which were common, so they had to find and train highly skilled pilots rather than the local drunks employed by the Jennings cartel. Luckily for Hillsinger and Quick, the Jennings locals thought their strategy so comically wrong-headed that they did not see the threat until it was too late.

In 1775, the war with England finally came, and it made Hillsinger and Quick fantastically rich. The family annalists went suspiciously dark during the war, a void that Wilkie found telling. No one hides the glory of his ancestors, he thought, and most invent it. One author leapt abruptly to the end of the war in 1783, when the firm's timber operation had without further comment been transformed into a hugely going concern (the word "firm" appears for the first time) called Hillsinger & Quick, Ltd, which suddenly boasted a fleet of fifty ships ranging from "light and fast timber haulers to decommissioned naval warships." This last point made the true nature of their business obvious—they were privateers. Elijah Hillsinger and Matthew Quick hunted British merchant ships, commandeered the cargo, and sold off the proceeds. It was the best real-world explanation for the conjunction of war, fast ships, outrageous success, and official gratitude, the last of which led to the grant of Seven Island.

For Wilkie, the unanswered question was why, of all things, they had asked for this particular archipelago when the American government decided to reward them. Less than three weeks after the ratification of the Treaty of Paris ended the Revolutionary War, the firm—not Elijah Hillsinger and Matthew Quick as individuals, but the incorporated firm of Hillsinger & Quick—had received, as a grant from the embryonic United States of America, not only Seven Island but also "any island dependency thereto that may be reached with a dry shirt at low tide."

If, Wilkie thought, the firm was so prompt to acquire this particular wilderness above all else, then there must have been a business problem that Seven alone uniquely solved. It was impossible that in acquiring Seven the two men were projecting their family's leisure needs forward one or two hundred years at a time when so many rational people, including George Washington himself, thought it was possible and even likely that the new republic would fail.

Wilkie imagined the partners expecting, or at least concerned about, a second war with an outraged and reloaded England, perhaps in league with an opportunistic naval power like the Spanish. The more Wilkie read, the more he believed that the Seven archipelago was, in effect, a palisade made out of tides. Cyrus had confirmed to Wilkie that, like the Jennings River, huge tides and unpredictable shallow points made the Seven thoroughfares especially dangerous for all but the smallest boats steered with the most complete local knowledge. Their fleet of unusual ships was designed to hide forever in the coves and rocks and murderous fog at the northeastern corner of the Seven archipelago, at the

43

meeting point of North and Pulpit and Sisters and Baffin islands, until the redcoats went away or were stupid enough to come in after them. Gaining official title to these islands, then, was a way to guarantee their business—and to some extent their lives—against the future atavism of the British Empire. If the archipelago threw off some timber or grazing, or if the children enjoyed the odd picnic there, then so much the better; but, Wilkie concluded, the logic of Hillsinger and Quick's vision had been wholly apocalyptic. Seven Island was a fortress built on auguries of eternal war.

11

Cyrus woke to see Sheila's face six inches away from his.

"There were three," Sheila said.

Martha was asleep next to him, so he pointed outside, and Sheila crept out of the room. The math was grim. If the ewe had produced multiple births, that would be a surprise and also a problem, since that particular ewe had two teats that were defective, out of four. At least one of the lambs must be dead, and given Sheila's inexperience, it was entirely possible that all three were gone.

"How many did we lose?" he said.

"None."

"Come again?"

"It's just that there were three."

"She's only got the two good teats."

"The third lamb is with Betsy."

Cyrus stopped outside the Staff House, which lay halfway between the small Manager's house and the barn.

"Betsy is a dog."

"She's nursing her own litter, so I just put the last one on her."

Betsy the Border collie had delivered six puppies less than a week ago. Cyrus had never heard of a dog nursing a sheep, but, on the other hand, the paths of grace are sometimes winding. If the lamb died, he could still say that everything possible had been done, that they had salvaged two head plus the mother from a hard pregnancy out of season. It was possible to transplant a newborn, so in theory one of the other sixty-odd ewes could have taken it on. That was labor-intensive, though, and it would have involved Sheila's waking someone up during the actual labor—which would have defeated the original purpose of keeping the experienced farmhands relatively fresh for the Migration. By that standard, Sheila's solution was fair.

Strictly speaking, the Migration was the annual stretch of time, started decades ago, when the Seven sheep were loaded onto a barge and released on North Island, at the archipelago's northeastern tip, where they grazed for eight weeks. The forage there contained a much greater concentration of clover, which was higher in protein than the grass on Seven proper, and that kept the sheep healthier over the long winters. From being a basic matter of animal husbandry, however, the Migration's meaning had over time evolved into something very different. When Cyrus formed his ministry—a congregation largely made up of current and former Seven staff—he'd obtained permission for the farmhands to suspend their work over that first thirty-six hours and hold a concurrent retreat on North, where there were three old shacks and a well. The retreat was dedicated to reflection, to spiritual work and teaching. It was a time of intensity and oneness, and Cyrus wanted his people awake and alert for it.

"You might have saved his life," Cyrus said to Sheila.

She began to cry just opposite the Staff House. She was young and she'd been up most of the night, so he let her go on for about fifteen seconds.

"That's enough," Cyrus said, and Sheila stopped.

12

Edward Peck, the boatman, opened his eyes and looked outside through the window. Everything was still. It was a little after dawn. The sky was overcast, but he predicted the gray would burn off into the perfect blue of the best days here.

Then something shifted through his peripheral vision. Peck sat all the way up. By the tree line, no more than fifty yards away, was a twelve-point—no—a fourteen-point stag, at least. He had never seen antlers on the Seven deer at all; this one had to be exceptionally strong to make it here. Peck reached under the bed for his old sniper's rifle, pulled back the bolt, and loaded it. He laid the rifle down on his bed and lifted the window as gently as if the beast were in the room—but when he tried to raise the screen, it jammed. Undeterred, Peck sighted along the barrel at the joint of the stag's left front leg, just below where he imagined its heart lay, to account for any deflection from firing through the screen.

The report was tremendous. Somehow he had forgotten that the gun would make a sound—and the crack echoed across the harbor and off the Indian Head cliffs opposite the family houses. The stag's left foreleg buckled right away, but he kept his balance until his right one collapsed too, followed by the rear. He fell heavily on his left side, just inside the tree line.

Edward Peck's first idea, as he ran out of the staff house, was to get the carcass as far as possible into the woods before anyone else saw it. He reckoned he could drag it a few hundred yards in, field-dress it, and then scatter the entrails for the crows before

47

hanging it from the hindquarters to get the blood out. He imagined that he would do all of this by himself. The woods back there were lightly traveled, so the stag should be safe tied up in a corner for a day or so. At that point, he would butcher it himself and present the meat to Cyrus as a gift. It was all possible—it was even excellent—but if he wanted to keep the head and neck, which he did, it was going to take speed and strength, right now. At the tree line, he knelt down to test the body's weight. Even just the head was shockingly heavy: his entire plan was impossible.

"Peck," Cyrus said from behind him.

Why is he awake already? Peck thought, even before turning around. He had already forgotten how loud the rifle shot had been.

"That's the stag been eating Mrs. Hillsinger's flowers," Peck said, risking a smile.

Cyrus laughed. He too knelt down and lifted its foreleg, and then let it fall.

"Shoot from the window?"

"Through the screen."

Cyrus whistled.

"Clean," Cyrus said, examining the wound. "Fourteen points. Don't see that much over here."

"Pretty lucky," Peck said.

"In the army, you'd get a medal for a shot like that."

"Can I keep the head?"

Cyrus smiled.

"You're on the first boat out," Cyrus said, "which is in seventy-two minutes. Leave an address on your bed for your last paycheck. Pack well—anything you leave behind will be sold or thrown in the fire."

Nothing in Cyrus's tone or bearing was angry or even agitated, and nothing announced that Peck was being fired. The emergence of the stag—so close by, and right when he'd opened his eyes—was such obvious good luck, such a clear case of a once-in-a-lifetime chance, that it would certainly merit an exception to the rules. Even Cyrus could not punish destiny.

"Can't shoot guns in the clearing," Cyrus said, "especially with the families here. That was all spelled out for you."

"You said it was a clean shot."

"So it was," Cyrus said, looking at his watch. "Boat leaves in seventy-one minutes."

Jim Hillsinger had been awake for hours when he heard the rifle, so he got up to see what was happening. He felt a sort of disorder at work within him, a lack of discipline to his thoughts. He hoped that air would help.

Lila had not come to bed. After the Old Man's rant about Baffin, she had left the living room, left the house, and not returned. That reaction was more than he'd expected, although he'd expected something. The Baffin idea had some merit, especially now that Catta was twelve. James was too old, and anyway he was too brittle for an opportunity like this. He would draw the wrong lessons. Hillsinger had observed that the margin between success and failure in his line of work was often a function of simple endurance. But how to teach it—endurance? He was not sure it was possible, but if it were, then the Baffin solution was a fair candidate. Lila, of course, did not agree. He hoped she had not done anything rash, which he defined as anything the Quicks might know about.

The sky was faintly pink when Hillsinger began to walk toward the tree line by the barn. Over there he could see two people talking, and—given that a gunshot in the clearing was very much against island rules—one of them would almost certainly be Cyrus.

Lila woke to the rifle shot. She was in the New House, and the pink sky outside the window told her it was already past time for her to be gone. She did not trust herself to replicate the staff's hospital corners, so she had not turned down the sheets or even unfolded the heavy wool blanket at the foot of the bed, and, luckily, it had not been cold overnight. Her sister, Hannah, had sometimes spent nights in one of these attic rooms—originally they were for the maids—rather than in her and Billy's much-grander usual room, with its four-poster bed and immense Shaker wardrobe, the one piece of New House furniture that Lila envied. Hannah was an early riser, while for some reason Billy, a man of regular habits in Manhattan, turned nocturnal on the island. He would get up and down and open all the creaky doors and sleep until noon, so Hannah had commandeered this little-used, unglamorous room as a solitary refuge.

Now Lila wanted to see her husband. She had slept here at the New House not so much to punish Jim as to insist upon the old contract. His work implied a certain violence, ran her understanding of their basic agreement, but that violence, such as it was, would be tightly compartmentalized. He would understand; he would say that Baffin was a fever dream of the Old Man's, a fantasy—an impossibility. He would promise. Lila walked downstairs and out without seeing or hearing any sign of the New House people. She had not seen Billy, nor felt anything at all here in his house, other than heavy sleep and the residue of her evaporating anger. Now she was outside, standing over the harbor, which every morning looked like it had been created just the night before. Everything was still.

And then her wish was answered: there was Jim, out on the lawn, walking toward her from the barn. He must have heard the rifle, too.

Lila kissed him lightly.

"It was the old talk," Jim said without preamble.

"Please say it."

"None of our children will set foot on Baffin Island."

He smiled, but Lila still felt somehow in the wrong, as if she had coerced him about Baffin. Which she had. Which had been essential.

"Why were you up?" she said.

"That rifle shot."

"It was loud."

"I had to talk Cyrus out of firing Edward Peck for shooting his gun in the clearing."

"Why you?" Lila said, laughing.

"Because Billy won't be up for hours."

"That was good of you—I like Edward Peck."

"And this," Jim said. "Cyrus said three lambs were born last night."

"Three! All at once?"

"In the barn. He said you should tell Isa."

Isa was her youngest, a gorgeous surprise. She was now six, and wholly preoccupied with the secret lives of animals.

"She'll die from happiness."

Then he was quiet.

"Please say you didn't sleep in the woods," Jim said.

"No," she said.

"Tell me."

"The New House attic."

He paused. "Ah."

"No one saw me," Lila said.

"That's good."

"It was the room Hannah slept in when Billy stayed up late," she said.

Lila was encouraged by his relatively easy responses. She might have overreacted last night, although she was not sorry.

Months ago, at home in Georgetown, a bedraggled man was handing out pamphlets near Dumbarton Oaks, which was odd because not many people walked by there. The man had shouted to her from across the street. Lila was startled, but she had stopped and looked at him. Encouraged, the man said it again: *millions now living will never die.* He seemed compelled to repeat it, as if the immortality of the chosen were only real while the words still lingered in the air. *Millions now living will never die,* he had said again before Lila moved on. Something in his phrase matched something in her mood that day, and it made her happy.

While sharing nothing else, Lila thought, this man and her husband both spoke from a very hot core of certainty. They were men of faith. From time to time, Jim would speak about something, the role of Portugal in NATO, say, or coal or medieval agriculture, and she would be transported, against her will—it had happened the night before, when Jim had silenced the Old Man. At those times, Lila thought, his voice became uncanny. She would feel entirely at peace. It had happened the night she met him, by the fountain at that party in Philadelphia, when all he'd said was that it wouldn't rain.

"I might go out on the boat today," Jim said, "to look at that eagles' nest Peck was talking about."

"I'm sure Catta would want to go with you," Lila said, for no other reason than her wish to hear Jim say Catta's name out loud.

"Good," Jim said. "I'll take him with me."

15

Catta woke up early, although later than he'd hoped: the sun was above Indian Head now, and the sky was already blue. His goal had been to leave the Cottage in the dark, just after Martha put the biscuits out under a towel, the first thing she did before going up the hill to cook breakfast for the adults. Martha came back later in the morning, when everyone was up and the tyranny of James was in full effect, to fix the children long trays full of eggs and bacon. She banged on a pot to wake up the stragglers. When it was just Martha and Catta, sometimes she gave him the special blueberry jam, which was only for the adults. Then, fortified, he would head out to the far reaches of the island, to walk the trails and the canyons. He wanted to know the woods better than anyone else, better even than his grandfather, who could not walk too far anymore but who knew how deep the springs were and why there were no owls on Seven. It was his grandfather's idea, too, to invite eagles to come and live here by offering them the carcasses of dead lambs, which they left stretched out at the rim of Bonner field.

Catta hoped that, once he had committed the entire island to memory, he could begin to walk at night. To build up to that would take some time, several summers at least. There was a record posted in the library for the fastest circumnavigation of Seven Island (six hours, thirty-three minutes), but his grandfather said he had never heard of anyone trekking all the way around the island at night, and certainly not without a flashlight.

Catta was slowly reducing what he carried with him, and someday he would know how to fish without a rod, light a fire without a match. He would see at night without a flashlight. He would know what to eat out in the woods or—better—he would go for days without eating. He was teaching himself to read the position of the sun and stars and the gradients on the island, what they meant for navigation, and where to find drinkable water (which the Old Man said was almost nowhere apart from the spring near the house). Catta wanted to see an owl to prove the Old Man wrong; it made him sad to think that owls would never come to Seven.

When he walked into the kitchen, Martha was kneading out biscuit dough on a long wooden cutting board. She took a short glass and pressed it through the dough to make biscuits, and when she knocked the discs from the glass onto the baking sheet, they made a little sound: *thock*.

"You should be in bed," Martha said without looking at him. "If you don't sleep, you won't grow, and then you'll be short and have a complex."

Catta stared at the dough left on the cutting board. Long sleep was impossible here. There was too much to do, and to wake with the others meant living in fear of James.

Martha turned away from him and smiled. They were good friends, she thought, but this one would suffer. *Them that want are always wanting*, a preacher had said to her once. He said some people are given things—one can do this and another that—but then this other one sees something that floats up there out of reach like a cloud. *Those are the damned*, the preacher had said. He had shown her how to put out her hands, even in the dark, how to feel for a heartbeat in the soft places. Catta didn't have God, as far as she could tell; none of the Hillsingers did. That preacher had a lot of God, and in the end he had broken on the rocks. Maybe he had too much.

When Martha turned off the faucet, she heard the faint grinding of stone on stone under the kitchen floor, and then she knew for sure that it was Catta who kept the little packet of strange things down there, wedged behind a loose brick. It was a long, thin packet of aluminum foil with fishing hooks, fishing line, matches, some gauze and bandages, iodine tablets, and two Indian arrowheads that were sharp. She had found it while trying to figure out how so many crickets got into the basement, and she hadn't known which of the children left it there.

Catta stowed his emergency kit in the waistband of his shorts. The biscuits were done when he came back to the kitchen and he was glad that Martha made a few extra-big ones, which he liked best. She cut one open and put the bright-orange Seven Island butter on it along with the special blueberry jam.

"Where are you going so early?" Martha said.

Then Catta saw Penny Quick sitting on the floor on the other side of the kitchen, eating a biscuit. He had been sure he was the only one up. She was about his age and the niece of Billy Quick, although her parents were not currently on Seven. There were often random children in the Cottage—the beds were almost always full, and occasionally Catta was told the other boys and girls were cousins. Sometimes they belonged to guests at one of the houses, and sometimes they were not explained at all. Catta had seen Penny walk into the woods by herself at least once, which made him think she was less useless than other girls who were not named Sheila.

"I'm going to Indian Head," Catta said to Martha, although he expected to go much farther.

"Get back for lunch, or your mother'll run frantic."

"Can I have a biscuit to carry?"

"No—your mother'll blame me for encouraging you. You come back and see her about lunch."

"Martha, you're a tough broad," Catta said.

Martha stared at him for a second, and then laughed until she had to sit down. Someone had said it in a movie Catta saw on television, and he was glad she laughed. Martha wiped her eyes, inadvertently marking her own face with flour.

"You got some stuff there," Catta said, handing her a towel, and then Martha shooed them both out of the kitchen because she did not care to have the Quick girl around while she was working. Penny Quick asked questions, and she was watching all the time. The alert ones were the most dangerous, and Martha had never seen her before last week. The only children she trusted were the ones she had known since they were babies, and not even all of them. No one in their right mind, she thought, would trust James Hillsinger, and Martha had given him his bottles as an infant.

Catta debated stealing into the Hill House to get food so he could hike past lunch, but that would take time. It was risky. His mother worried when he came home too late in the day, though his father and the Old Man liked it when he stayed out on the trails, even when he missed dinner.

He walked out the screen door and Penny Quick was already on the porch, finishing her biscuit.

"Where are you going?" Penny said.

"The woods," Catta said.

It was true, of course, although the woods were a multitude of different things—the kaleidoscope turned every day. Some days he had mastered them, or certain parts of them, other times he was scared, and still others he was sure the trees were speaking to him. Once or twice he exhaled, and he would have sworn the leaves shook. Sometimes he could see three turns ahead of him; sometimes he was lost, and he walked in widening circles until he found a trail or the ocean. Other times he felt known or marked in the bad way, cut off, cast out specifically by name.

"Can I come with you?" Penny said.

It was a hard question. If Penny came, she might see the part that was impossible to talk about and then that part would seem more real, and he would know it was not something he had imagined. But then the magic part might not happen if he was not alone.

"I bet you don't have food," she said.

"I just ate breakfast."

"I bet you don't have food for later."

She pulled a sack from under the porch stairs and showed him a sandwich wrapped in wax paper, a small flask, an apple, and three chocolate-chip cookies.

"Did Martha give you that?" he said.

She didn't answer, but she smiled. There was too much he did not know yet for him to share the woods with anyone. He could outrun her if he had to, though she would probably not follow him. If she did, he could lose her either on or off the trails.

"Come on," he said, choosing to be brave.

Catta started walking down the path that led by the harbor to the chapel, and Penny fell in behind him. Past the chapel lay the woods.

16

October 1955
Harlem, New York City

When the school's principal entered, Hannah Quick was sewing buttons onto a sock puppet. The sewing was more difficult than she had expected—she was never good at it, and out of practice—although Hannah was helped by the size of her belly. She was six months pregnant, and the thread and buttons rested conveniently there, as if on a shelf.

Something for you from the Board of Ed, the principal said.

Official communications were normally left in the pigeonholes in the faculty room, but in this case the principal had carried the letter in to her, using both hands as if it were fragile or dangerous.

Thank you, Mr. Decker, Hannah said. My hands are full just now, but I'll read it as soon as I can.

The principal was visibly disappointed. He must have had minor fantasies, she thought, of seeing her recant in tears once they showed her the instruments of torture.

I was asked to make sure you read it, the principal said.

I certainly will, Hannah said, as soon as I finish these sock puppets of global revolution.

The principal left. It was unwise to bait him—in the long run it could only hurt her—but still sometimes she could not help herself.

She already knew what the letter was. The New York City Board of Education was in the process of purging all teachers with any Communist past or inclination, and as it happened Hannah had joined the Communist Party for a little over a year when she first moved to Harlem in 1947. She was twenty-two at the time, recently married, and she and Billy were about to walk away from all their family and friends. Her consciousness was late in forming, perhaps, but Hannah had no doubts about her path. She had been complicit for far too long. When she announced where they were going, and why, there were scenes with her mother, with her father, with Lila. They would move only twenty blocks north.

Hannah was training to be a teacher; it was her Party contacts who had suggested the move to Harlem. The Party was a force in the union there. The Communists interpreted Marxism as a mandate for the most basic forms of racial equality, a view not shared by the NYC Board of Education, and they had been active in Harlem since the Depression. In Hannah's school, Communism meant access to the same textbooks and pencils as the children thirty blocks downtown, clean water in the water fountains, healthy and edible food for lunch. Everything was concrete here, and nothing abstract. It was as if she had emerged from shadow into light.

Billy did not think in these terms. He saw the world as a series of possibilities, of rich ambiguities, and not, as she did, as a struggle between good and evil. Justice was not an emotion for Billy, as it was for her. He understood her sense of mission, certainly. He appreciated her energy and the depth of her commitment. He asked how he could help, although he never went to a meeting and he was not interested in the Party per se. And yet, without her calling, without the nourishment of a small group of similar souls, and as a person entirely able to sleep at night in the face of de facto segregation and other outrages, Billy had still agreed to throw away his old world, to let his friendships go (an estranged brother was his only close family) and to start over with her in a place that meant nothing to him, and so much to her. He kept his job and really nothing else. It was, Hannah thought, the most romantic thing she could possibly imagine.

It did not go well. Her new colleagues, her students, once even an old lady she met on the street—everyone was absolutely brutal; they called *her a voyeur, a carpetbagger, a slumming rich girl, even a spy. She would smile back, which was an advantage—it surprised them—although she could do it only because they were right, and because she needed a job. Anyway, she asked them, wasn't a voyeur still better than a debutante? The local criminals took Billy's wallet nearly every week without even bothering to threaten him. It was often hard to see the larger truth: that they had this one life, and that it must mean something. Billy did not read the pamphlets or books; he did not believe in the slogans, but he did listen. He asked her pointed questions, and he accepted the answers. It was almost as if he trusted her to be the conscience for both of them. She was not worthy of that, but she tried—they both did—and very slowly their day-to-day improved. Billy helped a neighbor with an IRS problem, and word got around that the white guy who wore a tie every day knew about money. Almost overnight, he became the unofficial financial adviser for the neighborhood, including the criminals, whose tax dodges, Billy said, were far more ingenious than those he had seen farther downtown. He kept his wallet after that.*

The letter from the Board of Education would say that she should report to a building in Midtown on a certain date and time, and that she should bring with her documentation of any formal, professional, political, or any other affiliations with which she would like to acquaint the Board. At this meeting, she would be asked by a man named Martin Berg, a New York City prosecutor, if she was now or had at any time been a member of the Communist Party. Regardless of her answer, she would then be asked to name others known to her as Communists. Once the questions started, the forms of jeopardy were specific. Hannah could be fired for sedition—for having been a member of the Communist Party. She could be fired for perjury—if she said that she was not a member of the Communist Party when some unknown informant had named her. Or she could be fired for simple obfuscation—for refusing to name others. This was how Mr. Berg had already prosecuted many of her friends and colleagues, and Hannah was sure it was what he would do to her. His approach was perfectly legal—it had originated in the New York State Assembly with an abomination called the Feinberg Law that, on the face of it, banned treason from the civil service but had since been adapted as a weapon to beat Communism out of the schools. The law had been affirmed by the Supreme Court, so there was no longer any hope of rescue by a higher authority.

At those tribunals, the reckless or very ideological had in the past refused to answer any questions at all; those unfortunates had been suspended, pending further investigation. The investigation, then, would become a form of unpaid purgatory. A handful of those summoned had leapt into the waiting arms of their questioners and supplied the names of others. Some teachers had simply resigned in advance of an expected summons. Hannah and her friends saw these last as the very worst, even worse than the traitors, since their removal from the equation allowed the enemy to focus resources on fewer targets.

To say that Hannah had been insignificant to the Party would be an understatement; she was young and terrified, intimidated by the long-standing members, and she had barely spoken at the handful of meetings she had attended. When she had spoken, she was attacked. In the end, she realized, her critics were right: she saw the revolution as a metaphor or aspiration, or, at her most radical, as a simple improvement in one's day-to-day circumstances. She did not see the relevance of Moscow to Harlem. She had finally resigned, or rather just stopped coming, as the meetings became more and more focused on the ideas of Trotsky rather than the fundamentally non-world-historical needs of her students, such as new chalkboards. Then, as these Board of Ed tribunals began to attack teachers she knew, the open question was whether she, Hannah, had been completely invisible to the authorities, or only partly so. Now they knew the answer.

17

It was early afternoon when Billy Quick finally came downstairs. A message from his office contained extremely good
news: all metals prices in Japan had spiked due to a series of
unexpected riots in the copper mines there. Metals prices
all moved together during times of indiscriminate panic, so
this was an ideal opportunity for his firm to exit their
position in a struggling aluminum refinery outside Kyoto.
There were no telephones on Seven—that was one of its
charms—so Billy's office had enacted the emergency Seven
Island protocol—in the event of *bad* surprises they were to trade
immediately, while with *good* surprises they would set up the
logistics of the trade and then give him twenty-four hours to
respond before executing it. He was especially pleased that the
ancien régime communications system had worked. His office
had called the nearest public telephone, at the motel in Jennings,
and then the motel sent a driver to leave a message in Seven's
mainland mailbox and fly the red flag on the dock, which meant
urgent. Cyrus had collected the message that morning, and Billy
was rereading it on the porch when he saw his daughters walking up the hill.

"Good morning," Billy said.

"It's afternoon, Daddy," Ann said.

"Not in Kyoto."

Ann was always angry with him, but Barbara, his little one,
smiled whenever he spoke to her.

"Is it a picnic day?" he asked Barbara.

"Yes! Yes!" she said, and then her mouth opened extraordinarily wide, as if she were about to eat every picnic ever imagined.

"We can't have a *real* picnic," Ann said. "Edward Peck is taking the barge to North Island to practice for the Migration, so there's no one to drive us."

Billy thought Barbara might fall over from disappointment. Barbara loved picnics more than anything else and she could eat a chicken leg on a blanket on the lawn and be happy, whereas for Ann, the only picnic worth the effort involved taking a boat to the outer islands, which of course involved boats and staff and inordinate planning, none of which was feasible today due to the coming Migration.

"Well—this year the sheep will have to stay on Seven," he said, "because Barbara wants a picnic."

"No, Daddy!" Barbara said, alarmed, almost wailing. "The sheep need to eat clover! It's only on North Island!"

"And what has Clover done," Billy said, "that she should be eaten by sheep?"

Barbara was confused into silence, while Ann ignored him severely.

"Where's Penny?" he said to Ann.

There was a strange thought abroad in the land, Billy had gathered, an incorrect impression. The thought ran that since his bereavement, Billy had infinite free time and also a boundless need for company. This mistake had allowed Billy's extended family to make requests of him that would have otherwise been wholly inappropriate, such as his brother's depositing his daughter, Penny, with them on Seven for two weeks while he went to Europe.

"I saw her walking toward the woods with Catta Hillsinger," Ann said darkly.

Ann was still too young to have an informed opinion on anyone going anywhere with boys, but she disliked the woods. She thought they were dirty and barbaric and a place where animals were neither charming nor well-trained.

John Wilkie emerged from the Hill House, saw them across the lawn, and waved before heading off in the other direction.

"Wave to Mr. Wilkie," Billy said, and the girls waved furiously.

Wilkie stopped, ensnared by the waving children.

"We don't need a boat to have a picnic," Billy continued. "We'll go to the beach instead."

Barbara shrieked happily, and the girls went inside to prepare for the excursion. Wilkie was walking toward him over the lawn.

"Tell your father the news from Japan is good," Billy said.

"Aha," Wilkie said. "He'll be so pleased."

Peregrine Wilkie had money invested with Billy and, like most clients, he liked to hear good news.

"Come with us on the boat later," Billy said.

"I was told there were no boats today."

"Chairman's prerogative."

"That sounds fascist."

"Only if you're not the chairman."

Billy was feeling expansive, and this brief return of his good old rhythm with Wilkie reminded him of—and made him choose to forgive—Jim Hillsinger's harsh tone last night. It was usually wise to disregard anything said or done in that house after dinner, and anyway, given the circumstances, he could afford to be generous.

Lila had slept in the New House last night, although not with him. Billy was up late, as usual, and found an attic door left open that was normally closed. He had climbed the stairs, fearing possums, but instead, there was Lila curled up on top of the covers in one of the attic rooms.

Obviously, Hillsinger knew that Lila had slept elsewhere. He would be concerned, and Billy reckoned that she would tell her husband the truth. And, as truths went, the easy interpretations were mostly anodyne: she was missing Hannah, angry that Jim had mentioned Baffin, et cetera. On the other hand, it was not helpful for other men's wives to sleep in one's house alone, however innocent last night's reality might have been. It would help, Billy thought—it would be less dangerous for him personally—if Hillsinger heard the truth from Lila and then again from some disinterested third party. John Wilkie, for example, would be ideal. Billy knew better than most that Wilkie had terrible flaws—he was political in the bad sense and also fundamentally a coward—but, to his credit, he had deep and accurate instincts about information. He more or less made his living by deciding what certain people should or should not be told.

"If Hillsinger seems at all concerned," Billy said, "tell him that last night Lila slept in one of our old attic rooms."

"Aha," Wilkie said.

Billy could not tell from his face or tone whether Wilkie already knew this or thought anything in particular about it. Billy did know, however, that Wilkie valued information more highly than almost anything else.

"The attic door was standing open," Billy said, "which it never is, so I went up there to fight off the bats and raccoons. Lila was fast asleep on top of the covers in the room that Hannah slept in sometimes."

"I see."

"Use your judgment," Billy said to Wilkie, "but no need to tell Hillsinger, unless he seems concerned."

"Noted," Wilkie said.

"Hannah must have told her about that room."

"I'm sure she did."

"Don't forget—be on the dock at six o'clock sharp," Billy said.

"Actually," Wilkie said, "Lila said there was a formal dinner tonight. For the Migration?"

Billy paused.

"Christ—I completely forgot."

Catta stood at the top of the Indian Head cliffs and watched a gull attempt to fly while suspended in a strong headwind. He was so close that he could have leapt into the open air and touched it. He shouted and the gull turned and looked at him, and then went back to his struggle with the wind. Soon the gull worked free, dove downward into the shear, and then he was gone.

Through the hole where the bird had been, Catta saw the flat, red metallic barge, passing the bellbuoy and then turning to traverse the longest edge of the island toward the lonely corner of Seven that lay farthest from the clearing. Penny had stopped following him a little way into the woods and now she sat at the very front of the barge, her feet dangling in the whitecaps. Catta laughed out loud and shouted as loud as he could. They would never hear him, not at this height and distance, not against the wind and the motor. And then Penny's head spun around. She waved enormously with her whole arm, like someone drowning, and Catta was suddenly happy. He shouted again, and then he waved and Penny waved and Edward Peck waved, too. The barge disappeared around the corner, and Catta turned and hurried home for lunch, taking the trails for better speed.

Just before Wilkie left for Seven, his wife had asked him—had essentially demanded—that he ride a horse on the beach. Among the rock and penury of Northern Maine, it was a geological freak that there existed here a mile-long white-sand beach in a crescent shape, in a protected harbor facing the open sea. It was called the Long Beach. There were also stables with friendly horses available to ride. He had made the tactical error of telling Lucy both of these things, not knowing that his wife had one time ridden a horse on a beach, in Mozambique, and that for her it lingered as an enduring moment of bliss.

When he arrived on Seven, Wilkie dutifully told Lila that he would like to go riding. She was surprised, since she knew that John Wilkie hated both horses and riding, two notable facts that, apparently, he had not yet found the time to share with his relatively new and deeply equestrian wife. The mornings were unstructured here, and Wilkie was sure that in the end Lucy would enjoy the story of his attempt, even if it was mostly about his own abject fear of a miniature pony. Lila said to check in at the Staff House, where a farmhand told him to saddle the brown horse in the barn, and now Wilkie stood in front of six stalls containing six brown horses. It was possible that *saddle the brown horse* was a euphemism for something else.

Each stall had a chalkboard with a name on it. The name of the horse was important, because it was possible that, if his ride went especially badly, Hillsingers and Quicks alike would retell this story for a thousand years. The ideal horse would be named something neutral, after a shrub, for example, or some-one's maiden aunt. It would be unfortunate to die on a horse named *Cupcake*. A young farm girl named Sheila had been assigned to guide him, and she seemed to know the personalities of all the horses in outstanding and almost certainly fictitious detail. They settled on a brown mare named Maple.

Sheila walked both horses out of the barn and, since today the universe was clearly conspiring against him, they met Cyrus and three farmhands headed down the hill toward the dock. One did not like to look bad in front of Cyrus. Sheila mounted her horse in one motion, apparently assuming that Wilkie would need no help.

"Nicely done," Cyrus said to his niece.

There was no way for him to follow that particular act with this particular audience, and anyway, he wanted to tell Cyrus something.

"Cyrus, could I speak with you for a moment?" Wilkie said while Sheila rode her horse around them in tight, impressive, and wholly unnecessary circles.

"Careful, Mr. Wilkie—Maple there is a killer," Cyrus said as he waved the other farmhands down the hill. "How can I help you?"

Wilkie did not know exactly why Billy told him that Lila had slept at the New House last night. It was an important thing for Hillsinger to know, but it was also, Wilkie thought, the type of news whose messenger might be shot rather than thanked. He would pass it along and hope that it reached Hillsinger by some other route.

"This is just a touch sensitive," Wilkie said to Cyrus, using his voice of professional secrets. "Last night, Lila Hillsinger slept in Hannah's—the late Mrs. Quick's—old room in the New House."

71

"Her attic room," Cyrus said.

"I only mention it," Wilkie said, "because the anniversary of Hannah's passing is coming up. Small gestures might be especially welcome right now."

"Small gestures," Cyrus said, repeating.

"I mean some little thing for Lila," Wilkie said. "It could be anything—are there peonies on the island? They were Hannah's favorite."

"I'll check the garden."

"That's just one idea."

"I guess Martha could make summer pudding."

"There—fantastic. Thank you, Cyrus."

20

Jim Hillsinger dove into the harbor, bracing for the cold. The day was nearly perfect, bright and blue, and he watched the pines on Indian Head rise higher as he swam out. Coming around the orange buoy, it was essential to avoid the chain, which filtered all the tidal waste: seaweed and fish guts and God only knew what else.

As Hillsinger turned and headed back toward the houses, he saw Cyrus lifting the lid on the lobster pot next to the dock. Cyrus was fundamentally good at his job, which was to know everything happening on the island, and Larry Hott, the lobsterman, usually delivered his catch first thing in the morning. Which meant that Cyrus would already know the lobsters were there, and he was using them as a pretext. Cyrus had something to tell him. Hillsinger switched to freestyle and tried to look smooth on his last few strokes in to the dock. When he climbed the ladder, he was glad the sun was out.

"Good swim?" Cyrus said.

"You should try it," Hillsinger said.

"Maybe tomorrow."

"You say that every time."

"Always mean it, too."

"One day I'll get you out there."

Cyrus laughed.

There was a pause.

"Wanted to tell you," Cyrus said, "that we got a nice flat of berries in today from the mainland."

"Excellent."

"Martha thought she would make summer pudding for the Migration dinner tonight."

"That's kind of her," Hillsinger said. Something was going on here, but he could not yet tell what it was.

Summer pudding was a dessert of the invisible-hand school, stale bread left to soak with fresh berries and—if you were savage—sugar. Martha was entirely savage.

"Martha understands Mrs. Hillsinger's feeling poorly," Cyrus said.

"Say again?"

"Feeling the loss of Mrs. Quick."

"What gave her that impression?"

Cyrus paused, and looked out to the orange buoy.

"Sorry if we've been misinformed."

"Has Martha noticed a change?" Hillsinger said.

"Only her pilgrimage to Mrs. Quick's room in the New House," Cyrus said.

"Ah." There it was, Hillsinger thought. The story was out.

"Let her know that me and Martha feel the loss, too."

"Thank you, Cyrus," Hillsinger said.

Hillsinger turned and walked slowly up the ramp while buttoning his dry shirt on his wet torso. He had not brought a towel today due to the bright sun, and now he regretted it.

21

October 1955

Harlem, New York City

The letter from the Board of Education had said exactly what she thought it would say. She was to report to a certain building at nine A.M. *on the next Friday.*

There's no evidence, Hannah said. I put a ten-dollar bill in a jar— that was the annual dues. I barely said anything. Nothing was ever written down.

Doesn't matter, Billy said.

I can refuse to answer, Hannah said. I can sit there and be silent.

Doesn't matter, he said.

The mothers of my kids will write letters, Hannah said. They did it for Alice Citron.

The Board of Ed isn't people, Billy said. It's a machine.

A machine for what? Hannah said.

Billy shook his head.

The rain had started with a few scattered drops on the tin roof next door, like a handful of little stones. The speed and frequency increased, and soon it was raining hard. It is odd, Hannah thought, how rarely one hears thunder in the city. Their windows were still open and the rain muffled Billy's voice. The street sounds were muffled, too.

We can build an ark, Hannah said.

They both laughed. They did not hear the buzzer right away.

Their visitor was reduced to standing on the stoop in the torrential rain, ringing the bell every thirty seconds. He could see the light on in their apartment, so he knew they were home.

After ten minutes the rain let up slightly, and then, through the two glass doors, Billy was lumbering down the stairs.

Can I help you? Billy said automatically as he opened the door.

Billy, it's John Wilkie.

John!

They had not spoken in five years.

We should talk about Hannah's letter, Wilkie said.

What letter? Billy said.

The one from the Board of Education, Wilkie said.

How could you possibly know about that?

I won't keep you long, Wilkie said, and he entered and started up the stairs without being asked.

The Quicks' door, on the third floor, was standing open. Wilkie knocked in a pro forma way, and entered. Hannah was sitting at the small kitchen table.

John! Hannah said. What a nice surprise. Coffee will be ready in ten seconds.

It was an attractive thing about her, Wilkie thought, the unflappability. Hannah had openly disliked him; had conceived and carried out a monstrous and long-term excommunication of friends and family; had now added on to that, if the Board of Education was to be believed, the real possibility of sedition; and yet she maintained these unforced, crystalline manners. He felt very aware of his wet raincoat.

Let me take your mac, Hannah said, and when she stood Wilkie saw her very large belly. He had not known that she was pregnant. He wondered if Lila knew.

Congratulations, Wilkie said.

76

You find us overcome with blessings, Billy said, closing the door behind him.

A pause followed that, among friends, would have been awkward. However, since it was prelude to an explanation of Wilkie's unexpected visit, this particular silence was close, meaningful, alive. It was almost like intimacy.

In the silence, Hannah hung up his dripping coat on a rack on the landing, closed the door, and picked up the coffeepot.

Hannah, Wilkie said, I understand that you received a letter from the Board of Education.

Still milk and two sugars? Hannah said.

Yes, Wilkie said.

I received that letter just today, Hannah said.

She put a monogrammed silver tray on the small kitchen table, and poured the coffee into a china service that, Wilkie happened to know, was a wedding gift to them from Lila. He was surprised that she had kept it.

I was asked to come here to do two things, Wilkie said. First, to tell you what you should expect from the Board of Education hearing, if you choose to appear, and second, to offer you a better path than the one the Board of Ed wants you to travel.

Asked by whom? Hannah said.

By Peregrine Wilkie, he said.

I would have thought, Billy said, that this was a dangerous thing for your father to get involved in.

We take the world as we find it, Wilkie said. First, the Board of Education. The prosecutor will ask about—rather, he will announce— Hannah's membership in the Communist Party. Are you still a member?

No, Hannah said.

Are you currently active in the Party, Wilkie said, in any way?

No.

Did your family—other than Billy—know about your Party membership?

No.

Wilkie had his first sip of the coffee. Everything had depended on her answer to those three questions. Should Hannah have answered yes to any of them, he had explicit orders to leave the apartment immediately.

How did they find out? Hannah said.

The FBI is involved, Wilkie said, as are others with similar resources. The important thing to understand is that all Board of Education hearings are mandated to be public. In practice, then, once your name is listed on the docket at one of these hearings, it is in the papers. All of the papers. You are marked forever as a Communist. For the targets of the first prosecutions, I imagine that was not too much of an inconvenience; they were true believers and prepared for martyrdom. My understanding, though, is that Hannah's Party activity was incidental at best.

You have good information, Hannah said.

You mentioned an offer, Billy said.

I do have an offer, Wilkie said. Your path is narrow: there is only one good option. If Hannah allows her hearing to go forward, the ramifications will be wide and deep, starting with her termination or suspension, vilification in the papers, et cetera. Those consequences are merely personal. It's the other, collateral damage that you may not be aware of. If and when Hannah's Party membership becomes public—no matter how brief your participation—Billy will be fired from the bank immediately. That is not an opinion; it is a fact. It is possible that Jim Hillsinger will be fired from his job as well. But the most serious impact, Hannah—and, really, the one that brings me out here tonight—will be on your father. He has the farthest to fall. The chairman of the board of Chemical Bank, we happen to know, is under consideration for Secretary of the Treasury, if and when Johnson wins the election in November. The chairman will be forced to take strong measures against anyone at the bank with Communist ties, meaning that, should this news become public, Mr. Blackwell will be summarily expelled from the Chemical Bank Board. He will then be prosecuted by Chemical Bank for something, anything, in order to make the separation more vivid. Again, this is not my opinion—contingency plans already exist. The charge in these cases is usually misappropriation of funds. Mr. Blackwell will then be removed from all directorships, club memberships, everything. He and your mother will be completely isolated.

Hannah's lovely equilibrium had now vanished. She did not have Lila's beauty or sheer presence, nor the sense of outrageous holiday that Lila could sometimes command, but just now Hannah had a quality, an absolute contempt for the world, that, for obvious reasons, he had not seen at the round of engagement parties or the wedding or the silly lunches. He liked this version better.

As you know, Wilkie continued, Peregrine Wilkie is also a member of the Chemical Bank Board. He is, in fact, the head of the Standards Committee, and in that role it would fall to him to prosecute Mr. Blackwell. My father does not want to do this.

In your opinion, John, Hannah said, is any of this is reasonable?

No, Wilkie said. It's an abomination. But the Supreme Court has affirmed the Feinberg Law, which is the basis for all this unpleasantness. The law may change at some point, but not before tomorrow.

What if I make a strong stand? Hannah said.

There is no stand to make, Wilkie said. You're already guilty in the eyes of the law. This is not a trial, nor is it an investigation, and least of all is it a debate. It's a public hanging. There is exactly one outcome that we can still prevent, and that is keeping Hannah's name off their docket. Once her name is printed, nothing else matters.

What are you proposing? Billy said.

79

My father, Wilkie said, *has directed me to tell you that he is prepared to make a sizable personal investment into a new fund created under Billy's sole direction, and he will further recruit no less than five other substantial investors, including your soon-to-be-former employer. In short, my father will guarantee the following things: first, Billy's graceful exit from his current post; second, your family's immediate financial security, as well as the fund-raising and legal work to set up Billy's fund; and, third, the safeguarding of Mr. Blackwell's position both in the bank and in society, insofar as that's possible. He will do all of this only if Hannah officially resigns from her teaching post* tomorrow—*the hearing docket goes to the printer the day after that, and the newspapers are in the habit of stealing proofs from the printer's garbage cans.*

Does my family know you're here? Hannah said.

No, Wilkie said.

Who else knows you're here?

The bare minimum.

All I do every day, John, Hannah said, *is show children how to write in cursive.*

Exactly, Wilkie said, rising from his chair. *Only a dangerous and determined Communist—only the most committed revolutionary intent on the violent overthrow of the government of the United States—only that person would be willing and able to do such a mundane thing as to teach cursive for as long as you've done it, and in such an unforgiving place. That is what the prosecutor and the papers will say. And if you listen to nothing else I say, please understand that these people have already won.*

22

Hillsinger entered the house through the kitchen door and climbed the back staircase. He needed time, and the children's play area, which was at the top of the stairs, would be empty now. Two small bedrooms were attached to it, and Hillsinger shut himself into one of them and sat down on the floor. That Cyrus knew about Lila's night in the New House was disturbing, but really it only pointed toward the much larger problem of whether or not Billy Quick knew.

It was uncomfortable to be vulnerable to Billy Quick in any way, but especially so now. Hillsinger had known Billy since they were boys, from the Cottage on Seven, and he had always thought Billy was vague, insubstantial, lacking in depth. As far as Hillsinger recalled their overlap on Seven, Billy usually opted out of the Indian Game, and the result of that abdication was that he had no allies and no enemies. He was Switzerland, and nobody trusts the Swiss. Billy was graceful in a physical way, sort of, so one did sometimes remember things that he *did*—the way he played tennis, for example, or how he smoked—but his mind was third-rate at best. One could never recall what Billy *said*. He had grown up in several different places before his family settled in New York during the War, and whether one chose to view his particular type of sophistication as attractive or irritating depended on whether or not Billy was in a position to hurt you. For a long time, he was not.

The Blackwells had taken the four of them—Billy, Hannah, Lila, and himself—to Round Hill for a few days during that brief, sunlit period after he and Lila were engaged but before Hannah had cut ties with the family. Per usual, Jim rose early and played tennis badly; he sat on the bleachers afterward, while Billy went on the court with a man they had all met at dinner the night before. The man's name was Montague. Billy was a remarkably elegant tennis player, but Montague looked as though he could have played professionally. He was on another level. Each of Montague's shots, however, that was clearly in but within an inch or two of the line, Billy called *out*. He did this repeatedly, and Jim watched them for twenty more minutes, just to be sure. It was appalling, and, worse, it made no sense, since even with the unfair advantage Billy had no chance.

You cheat at tennis, Hillsinger had said to him at lunch that day, before the others arrived. He made it into a joke.

Hardly, Billy had said, matching his tone. *I'm nearsighted*. It was a quirk of Billy's normal speaking voice that he could sound both serious and ironic at the same time, so Hillsinger was left with no idea whether or not Billy was denying the charges.

In his early career, Billy had not played for the same high stakes that Hillsinger had, and certainly where he had first landed, at a big bank, he stood no chance of being promoted with Hannah's politics being what they were. But the Board of Education witch hunt had forced Billy to leave and start his own company, an investment fund focused abroad, and the active support of Peregrine Wilkie had made his business secure. More surprisingly, in the quiet rooms where old men decided where the real money would go—Hillsinger himself had seen them, during his Wall Street interlude before the CIA—Billy's relative isolation came to be seen as a strength. He invested in exotic, difficult markets like Japan and Angola, and *exotic* was certainly not the old men's favorite word. However, with a nudge from Peregrine, they began to note that Billy's fund was mostly uncorrelated to the U.S. market, which they said made their overall portfolio safer. And so Billy became their favorite hedge against domestic catastrophe. His timing was also good because fortunes were being made in obscure corners of the market, and the old men liked fortunes. The trickle of funds increased to a healthy flow, and finally Billy ran enough money, from enough different people, that he became both rich and astonishingly well connected. He became dangerous.

The absurd and stinging part was that their former roles were now more or less reversed. Hillsinger had always stood at what seemed like the center of the world, in the sense that the people he knew and the institutions in which he routinely thrived had the quasi-magical ability to change perception and even reality. They could make careers, make money, change public opinion. After the War, for example, they called the CIA the great slaughterhouse: the place in America where the best men were separated out from the merely very good. For a long time, Hillsinger had been among the best.

In the CIA's infancy, he was handpicked by Director Dulles and installed temporarily on Wall Street while Congress built the nation's intelligence apparatus. When Hillsinger was finally summoned to Washington, they were not called the CIA, their office was in a broken trailer on the Mall, and for two years they did not have typewriters or even stationery. The Soviets had obliterated them at first. News of fresh disaster came nearly every day, and many men died. Between 1947 and 1949, they had lost at least two hundred in Albania alone. But eventually they learned, and once they did—once they had not only understood but truly *absorbed* the stakes—then they were more than good. For two years Hillsinger was on the front lines, in Warsaw, where he exposed three substantial KGB operations and where, by the end, the local Russians were legitimately afraid of him. He was recalled because the Director wanted him closer at hand, and when that happened they gave Hillsinger all the secret decorations that mattered, the ones that were never spoken of—majestic letters for his file. From that point on, he was marked: he would be Director, Ambassador to Paris, even Secretary of State. It was, they said over and over again, only a matter of time.

But then he—the same Jim Hillsinger—was accused of treason and forced to resign from the CIA. Only five men knew of the treason charge and four of them did not believe it, but the odd man out was James Angleton, the head of Counterintelligence, who was adamant. The Director gave Angleton what he wanted, and Hillsinger had gone quietly, the way the innocent always did. The charge would never be public or even known beyond that small circle, although it would also never be *dis*proven. Not officially. Among those who knew, the stain would never completely fade.

So what now? How to live, when a calling was revoked? What could compare? He was tempted to say *nothing*, but then there also was, in one dark corner of his brain, something else— an intimation. A possibility of rebirth. The idea of emerging from this disaster, in another city, as someone else—someone leaner, more austere, stripped of his last unhelpful illusions— very few people get that type of chance. He intended to take advantage. But before he could do that, he would have to understand very precisely how he had been tricked so many times, and on such a large scale. Because for all of this to have happened—and for it to have happened to *him*, of all people— *he must have been told lies that he wanted to believe.*

23

Lila's youngest, little Isa, had asked why they built fairy houses only out of things that were on the ground. The things they used, Isa said, like bark and pinecones, fell apart so quickly; the fairy house they built just yesterday had already collapsed. Lila nodded sympathetically; she had asked herself the same question. They never ate food that fell on the ground, Isa had continued, so why did fairies want branches and leaves for a roof instead of shiny and smooth things like her rain hat, which she had carried out from the house even though the weather was beautiful? The truth, of course, was that the Old Man had decreed it so.

Fairies, Lila had said to her daughter, *are different from us. They are so pure that they don't see dirt. All they see is a pinecone that had once been part of their friend the pine tree, or bits of soil shaken loose from their friend the Earth. Above all things*, she said, *fairies want to be among their friends.*

"But what do fairies eat?" Isa said for the thousandth time.

"Fairies eat the sunlight," Lila said yet again.

Isa paused.

"What if it rains?"

Up to that point, Lila felt they were in the domain of ritual, and she was content to answer, as many times as necessary, in that spirit. But this was a new question.

"If it rains," Lila said hopefully, "then they eat clouds."

"Is that why the sun comes back again?"

Lila smiled, but chose not to answer. The logic of fairies, if pursued too far, could end up in a scary place.

All these houses were tiny, a foot high at most, and designed as resting places for fairies who were pictured by the children, as far as Lila could tell, as fireflies with human features. The houses lined either side of the road as it entered the forest from the clearing, and the Old Man would remove *non-Seven* items—anything with manmade building materials—from offending fairy houses and pile them on the Hill House front steps as a warning. Spoons for gateposts or eyeglasses for windows, cigarettes for seesaws or the Stork Club ashtray used for a swimming pool. All anathema. It was astonishing, Lila thought, how even this flimsiest of pastimes, when repeated enough, could evolve such a tangled and specific set of rules.

Lila was searching the underbrush for a square patch of moss to use as a roof or perhaps a doormat, when she heard Isa shriek.

"Catta!"

The fairy houses were one of the six-year-old Isa's two main preoccupations on the island: the other was Catta. She was thorough in documenting and "treating" all of her brother's perpetual cuts and bruises. When he sat down in her sight, Isa would examine his exposed skin for any new wounds and then put a Band-Aid on everything she could find, including mosquito bites, and his arms became a mosaic of bandages. The Hill House chronically ran short of medical supplies. Catta would take them all off after Isa went to bed, and at first Lila worried that, the next morning, the disappearance of Isa's careful work would make her feel rejected, but in fact she was delighted and cheerfully bandaged him up all over again.

"We made a fairy house out of birch bark!" Isa said as Catta walked up.

"It needs a roof, silly," Catta said. He lifted Isa up and turned her upside down and she shrieked again, and louder.

Back on her feet, Isa staggered briefly, dizzy, and then said that Mommy was just over there, finding moss for a roof.

"Will these help?" he said, and pulled four large feathers out of his waistband.

"Feathers!" Isa said, as if she had never seen anything so perfect.

"Those are eagle feathers," Catta said. So he hoped—it was hard to know which feathers belonged to which birds. The biggest and most symmetrical ones must, he thought, have come from eagles.

Isa laid the feathers lengthwise on top of the birch-bark walls, and they fit the house almost perfectly once Catta added a long, skinny twig as a crossbeam.

"Isa, think of how high up in the air those feathers have been," Lila said, returning empty-handed.

There had been no moss that was right for a roof or a doormat, which was disappointing, although she was pleased that Catta had come back for lunch. Sometimes he wandered all day, and then she worried. Lila decided that her worries from last night, spurred by Diana's doom mongering, had all been ridiculous. Just now he was very much a boy, and the three of them knelt down and placed fallen leaves into the gaps in the roof that the feathers did not quite cover.

24

Cyrus took a hammer and spike and thirty yards of rope to the tree line in back of the Staff House. He and his two sons dragged the stag's carcass into the woods, looking for a remote place to hang it, but it was so heavy they couldn't get it all the way off the ground and had to stop when the roots and brush grew too thick. They were closer to the clearing than Cyrus wanted, but it was good enough. There were no trails for a hundred yards in any direction. Matthew and Mark held up the stag's hind legs while Cyrus measured the rope into two equal parts and ran both lengths over a thick branch high up in the tree. He tied each leg with strong knots above the hoof, and then all three of them grabbed the rope ends and walked backward, slowly hoisting until the beast hung about two feet off the ground. Cyrus let go and his sons struggled to keep the stag aloft while he drove the spike into the tree at waist height. Then he tied off the ropes onto the spike. He shoved the carcass to test the rig. It would hold. He cut the stag's throat, to keep the meat tender for the Migration feast. The venison would be a nice surprise, and the blood now pooling would vanish by tomorrow morning. Sooner if they got a heavy dew.

25

Martha was disgusted. With the Migration coming tomorrow, with both houses full and the Cottage overrun by children, Jim Hillsinger had come into the kitchen and asked her to make eggs-in-a-basket for lunch today. That was Catta's favorite, on top of the summer pudding Cyrus had suggested for tonight. The special requests were multiplying too fast for her to keep up with her day-to-day work, but she agreed. You always agreed.

Eggs-in-a-basket were simple enough to make, although timing was crucial. They had to be hot rather than warm, which in practice meant that everyone must be seated before the cooking started. Just before one o'clock, she asked Susan who of the family was in the house. Susan didn't know. Martha was unimpressed by that answer, and she said so. Susan ran out of the kitchen to scout while Martha began the fried potatoes, which could be made in advance along with the asparagus.

The kitchen door opened behind her and Martha, focused entirely on shaking the correct amount of salt onto the potatoes, assumed it was Susan and did not turn around. She said, impatiently:

"Well?"

"Hello, Martha," Diana Hillsinger said.

This was a terrible sign—two family members in the kitchen on the same day. Martha predicted that, somehow, she would be awake well past midnight.

"I beg your pardon," Martha said. "I thought you were Susan."

Other staff members found this one trying—she was whimsical and changed her mind often, which led to more work. But Martha remembered her as a child, when Diana had brought flowers into the kitchen for her on three consecutive mornings. The fourth day, when it was raining, she brought a toad.

"I just wanted to ask you," Diana said, "to be extra mindful of the amount of salt you put in Jim's food."

"The amount of salt," Martha repeated to make sure she had heard right.

"It's bad for his blood pressure," Diana said.

"Mr. Hillsinger the younger?"

"My father is too far gone for it to matter."

Martha held up the tin saltshaker for Diana to see, and very deliberately put it on the shelf.

"Thank you, Martha," Diana said, and she exited back through the swinging door. Martha had gotten away easy, and she salted the potatoes anyway.

Before breakfast, Diana had walked down the hill to the chapel by the water, which was a short walk from the house. Her prayers came quicker there. Above all, she had asked for endurance, for her empathy to be equal to whatever agony was coming toward them.

She was overcome this morning with a terrible sense of foreboding, as if something black were hidden inside this gorgeous day. One could not know in advance what exactly her intuition was or what it meant—one could only react once the catastrophe revealed itself. Taking *some* action now, though, was better than doing nothing. She had wavered at the kitchen's swinging doors and almost turned around, but then the saltshaker had presented itself. Martha would think she was difficult—all the staff did—but it was possible she had removed at least one boulder from the coming avalanche.

Everyone was very late for lunch. Diana closed her eyes and waited.

26

Billy Quick was reading a letter from his distant cousin Charlotte. It informed him that Charlotte's sister Elizabeth and her alcoholic husband had been in a serious car accident three weeks before. The letter had come in the same packet as his Japanese message, but, dreading all communication from Charlotte, he'd put it aside until just now. Elizabeth was one of his favorites, but she had always been a poor judge of men.

She and the husband were recovering, but they'd be hospitalized for another month at least. Cousin Charlotte had been staying with their son, George, out in Denver, but now she had to go home. She was flying the unfortunate child from Denver to Boston, where she lived, but since it was impossible for her to accompany him to Maine, she would on such and such a day put the child on the train to Jennings by himself. She knew, Charlotte wrote, that Billy was on Seven for the rest of the summer and would want to help out. Billy compared the kitchen calendar to the dates she mentioned, and he realized that the letter was dated two weeks ago. He was receiving this itinerary on the morning of the evening that the boy was arriving at the train station.

Charlotte went on to say that hopefully he would not have George for more than two weeks and that surely he, Billy, would agree that sharing this burden was appropriate.

Why not? Billy thought. *The more the merrier.*

Billy finished his breakfast while the table was being set for lunch and then walked down to the workshop to tell Cyrus that, despite the Migration tomorrow, someone would have to go to the mainland tonight to collect young George. They would also have to make sure that the Cottage had a free bed to accommodate one more little savage.

27

It was more than laughter—it was almost thunder. Wilkie hesitated in the hallway until the roar died down. When he could only hear Jim Hillsinger's low voice speaking, he walked into the dining room where the Hillsinger nuclear family, plus Diana, was finishing their lunch at the massive oak table. Hillsinger was at the head, facing him, and continued to tell the joke:

"'I don't know,' the waitress said. 'I've never caught a rabbit myself.'"

There was another shout of laughter—even Diana laughed, which was rare. The children were nearly hyperventilating.

"Wilkie!" Hillsinger said, not waiting for the noise to fall away. "How was your ride?"

"Incredibly dangerous," Wilkie said.

"I'm afraid we started without you," Lila said.

She asked Susan to set another place.

"I could hear you all the way out by the barn," Wilkie said.

"This man," Lila said, pointing at her husband, "has been saying absolutely shocking things to the children."

Faux-disciplinarian was one of the recurring characters that Lila played from time to time, though neither Jim nor the children seemed to take it very seriously. Wilkie knew Lila's moods well enough to tell that she was delighted.

It struck Lila that Wilkie was about to see something different—her family in full-on carnival mode. She was not sure that was a good thing. From time to time and entirely without warning, Jim would launch into these states of exception, where the normal rules were suspended for hours or days, or longer: he would hold court, as he was doing now, assessing fines to be paid in jumping-jacks, impersonating forgetful elephants, serving ice cream for breakfast, pulling the children out of school to go on trips, to caves full of stalactites or a tunnel hidden under some Civil War mansion. Lila never knew how long the festival would last—nor, she thought, did Jim. Once it took hold, the children would vibrate with expectation because nearly every minute held some preposterous surprise—until Jim's chaotic energy ebbed away, or work intervened. Then the family abruptly went back to their normal, nonhilarious life. The transitions in and out were hardest on James, who cared the most about rules.

Today there was no preamble at all—Jim had simply started telling racy jokes there in the middle of lunch. James ignored him rather aggressively at first, eating four eggs-in-a-baskets and asking for more while his father was talking. However, once James saw Catta transfixed by the story, he began to listen, and then he committed entirely when he realized that the joke, which was long, was traveling far outside the normal decorum of the Hill House. Jim was never happy with small triumphs, so of course he launched immediately into a second one, about the waitress and three French soldiers. The sudden change caused madness in the children: tears streamed down Catta's face and James rocked back in his ancient side chair, laughing uncontrollably, until he fell back and the chair smashed to pieces on the floor. Catta laughed so hard that he began to choke. Some combination of Catta's laughing and coughing made James laugh harder still, and then the loving butterfly that was Isa wanted so much to laugh along with her brothers, to be a part of their outlandish game, that she threw up her arms in

95

fellowship, spilling an entire glass of cold milk into her lap. It made her shriek, which threw the boys into such primeval hysterics again, that for a moment Isa thought she was the luckiest girl in the world, to have inspired such a riot. This had happened just before Wilkie walked in.

Lila's eyes rested on her husband as Wilkie outlined the comic history of his fear of horses, including the terror unleashed by his slow ride on the beach on a ten-year-old horse named Maple. Jim glanced at her and covered her hand with his. His expression, Lila thought, said, *look around you—we have done all this.* It was familiar—it was perfect—and as the children's laughter swelled and broke, she thought about the architecture of this moment—how none of it could have been predicted at their chance meeting by the fountain in Philadelphia so many years ago. How fate had intervened.

"James," Lila said, "finish your asparagus."

28

March 1960

Harlem, New York City

Since leaving her school in Harlem, Hannah Quick had worked part-time as the secretary to a local patroness of left-leaning causes. Her days were engaged but boring, consisting primarily of sending money to various Civil Rights groups in Southern states. From time to time she ran into friends or acquaintances from the school, and among the scattered gossip was the odd fact that Bobby Sheppard, a sometime substitute teacher at the school, had recently disappeared. He had missed an entire week of a planned substitute engagement, all the while being unreachable at home. People had been worried. Sheppard was also a cartoonist for a local weekly, and it was assumed that something journalistic had pulled him out of town on short notice, but the paper's staff had no idea where he was either. And then Bobby Sheppard had turned up in East Berlin, as a defector.

Apparently he thought someone was after him, the colleague had said.

He was slightly touched, Hannah had said.

Two days later, Hannah was at home with the girls, now two and four years old. When Billy came home, she was roasting a chicken.

There are two men downstairs, Billy said when he walked in the door. They want to speak with you.

Who are they?

The FBI, Billy said. They want to talk about Bobby Sheppard.

The men from the FBI were almost excessively polite. Only one of them spoke, and that one said several times how good the chicken smelled.

She invited them both to stay for dinner, but they declined. Hannah said the truth: she knew Bobby Sheppard only in passing, as a substitute teacher at her school. They had an occasional chat in the teachers' lounge. She knew his cartoons in the Lennox Weekly. That was all.

They asked Billy if he had ever met Bobby Sheppard.

No, he said.

Would you be surprised, the FBI man said, to learn that Bobby Sheppard had defected to East Germany?

I was told that by an acquaintance last week, Hannah said.

Which acquaintance? the FBI man said.

She told them. If they were here talking to Hannah, then she was relatively sure that every teacher at the school would be on their list, too.

Among Sheppard's papers, the FBI man said, handing her a piece of paper, was this sketch from the faculty lounge at the school. You are in it, along with a number of others.

Is this meant to be me? Hannah said as she looked at the sketch.

The names are there in the caption, the FBI man said. It's notable that the other teachers pictured were all removed from work under suspicion of subversive activity. Do you know anything about that?

Hannah looked at the sketch again. The others were the teachers who were, as John Wilkie had put it the night he came to their house, the true believers. The martyrs. They were also her friends.

I certainly knew they were removed, Hannah said.

And you yourself, the FBI man said, resigned prior to testifying at a Board of Ed hearing. Is that correct?

I was six months pregnant at the time, Hannah said. I resigned prior to testifying to my own fertility.

And now you have two children?

Yes.

Congratulations.

Thank you, Hannah said.

The FBI man seemed nervous and highly scripted, as if he were conducting a polite conversation based on the principles of a book he'd read on the subject.

Mrs. Quick, have you ever heard the name Hans Kallenbach?

No.

This man Kallenbach, the FBI man said, seems to have been a benefactor of not only Bobby Sheppard, but also several people in that sketch.

How do you mean? Hannah said.

He seems, the man said, to have contributed meaningful sums of cash to the defense and living expenses of those concerned.

Surely charity is not a crime? Hannah said.

No, ma'am, said the FBI man. But will you let us know if in your travels you hear Kallenbach's name come up in any context?

Of course I will, Hannah said.

The FBI man complimented her chicken again, and the two men left. Hannah thought the encounter had gone as well as could be expected.

Maybe not, Billy said. Hans Kallenbach is one of my investors.

Who is he?

His family has a bank in Switzerland, and in New York he handles money for very rich people that, on the back end, he invests with people like me. We have lunch twice a year at that Hungarian place on Third Avenue. Peregrine Wilkie introduced him. He invested with me at the very beginning.

How would he know Bobby Sheppard?

No idea, Billy said.

Anyway, they missed it.

Let's hope so, Billy said.

29

Catta boarded the *Heron* along with his father, James, and the Old Man. He had already leapt onto his preferred seat up on the bow when Cyrus said, "Big bodies fore, small bodies aft." That meant the tide was very low, and Catta walked reluctantly back into the stern.

His grandfather did not normally go out on the boats, and the Old Man's presence today made the trip feel like a special occasion. Catta wanted to tell him about seeing Penny and the barge from the Indian Head cliff—how he had shouted and they had heard him from so far out on the water. How the gull had been only just there, just a few feet away, a prisoner of the wind. But for some reason, he could not find a way to start or a reason to pull his grandfather aside. He decided he would wait until they came back to the dock. The boat pulled slowly out of the harbor, and his grandfather stood next to the wheel, pointing out to Cyrus a series of invisible eddies surrounding imaginary rocks. Cyrus nodded each time and turned the wheel.

The part of Baffin where Edward Peck had seen the nest was across the channel from the old lumber camp at Starks Cove, and if for some reason they missed the eagles today, Catta thought he would look for them tomorrow from the Seven side. He would ask the Old Man for his binoculars.

When they reached the harbor bellbuoy, Cyrus looked over his shoulder. Then he looked again. He lifted the storage bench by the wheel, checked inside for a moment, and then abruptly turned the boat around.

"Why are we turning?" his father called out from the foredeck.

"We're short one life jacket," Cyrus said. "I didn't realize young James was coming along."

"We can do without it. Everyone here can swim."

"It's the law, especially with children on board. Peck says the Coast Guard is out today."

Back at the dock, Cyrus landed the boat so gently, and at such a good angle, that it stopped the instant it touched wood. James jumped out and stood on the dock, holding the bowline and waiting for instructions. Cyrus left the boat and walked up the ramp. After what seemed like a long time, he came back with his familiar battered sun hat, plus three more life jackets. Catta saw Martha walking uphill, away from the shop on the bulwark. He waved, but her back was turned.

"Anything else?" his father said to Cyrus, who shook his head and started the engine.

Catta was looking the other way when there was a rapid sound of feet on the metal ramp. As he turned, Penny Quick grabbed hold of the railing and vaulted onto the deck. She sat down in the center of the bow with her legs dangling over, laughing.

"Where are we going?" Penny said to nobody.

"To see the eagles," Catta said from the stern.

"Who is this?" his father said to Cyrus.

"She's Billy Quick's niece," Cyrus said. "I guess everyone wants to see the eagles' nest."

"Shouldn't she be in the stern?" the Old Man said.

"Nah, the balance feels about right just now."

The *Heron* pulled away from the dock and then when they entered the channel that ran along the island, Cyrus opened the throttle. Once they were at speed, he took off his sun hat and handed it back to Catta.

"Put that on," Cyrus said.

Catta looked up and the sun was behind a cloud, but one did not contradict Cyrus on boats. The hat was much too big: the band scratched him, and he had to hold on with one hand to keep it from flying off in the wind.

Hillsinger saw they were close to the open sea, and now the water was rougher. The boat rose and slammed down onto the whitecaps, but the Quick girl stayed up on the bow, drenched but not about to move.

After this morning's conversation with Cyrus, Hillsinger had decided, once and for all, to put Catta on Baffin for the night. He had promised Lila not to do it, but much had changed there in that little room off the back stairs. He had put all his assumptions to the torch. It was immensely unpleasant, but he had been blessed with luck or insight and now he knew where and what the lie was. The world was very different now from what he had thought—his marriage, the charges against him, his sense of a higher logic, and even his children, all were irretrievably changed. He had been blind, but now, standing here on the bow of the *Heron*, the world was brighter and sharper. Now he was free to act.

As far as Baffin was concerned, he was not deluding himself; he knew that Catta would suffer. Time moves slowly for children, and his hours on the island would feel like days, possibly even years. Catta would learn something about endurance, and he, Hillsinger, would find out precisely what was in his son. Lila would not like it, but he was sure she would accept it.

Back in the stern, Catta chose not to look at the mainland, which was off to his left. If you looked at the mainland, the kids said, the end of your trip came quicker. He focused on the woods instead. The woods had the power to slow time and expand space. When he was hiking off the trails, the idea that a forest might ever end seemed like a mistake or a lie, even when he could see the ocean through the trees.

His father walked back and sat next to him. He was quiet for so long that Catta assumed he was intending to be silent, which he sometimes did. At home his father would come into Catta's room and sit without speaking for long stretches of time, as if he were debating inwardly, or the two of them were somehow engaged in a collective meditation, like Quakers.

"We're going to Baffin," his father said.

"Do you think we'll see eagles?" Catta said.

It was obvious to Hillsinger that Catta was hoping for an answer that was not *maybe*. He had already asked the same question three times. Catta looked up and smiled, seemingly alive to his own absurdity, and that flicker of self-awareness made Hillsinger hope that the boy might be so instinctively farsighted, so intuitive, that without being told he would see the deeper underpinnings of what was about to happen. It was not fair, he knew, but Hillsinger let himself hope that his son was a freak of nature, or a magician.

"Do you know how to tell time without a watch?" Hillsinger said.

"No."

"First thing—determine south."

"Spain is there, so that's east," Catta said, rotating forty-five degrees. "South is there."

The Old Man had told him that, allowing for the curvature of the earth, Spain lay on a straight line across the Atlantic from Seven Island.

"Spain is there," Hillsinger said. "Zero degree, directly over-head, is noon. Now we divide the sky into eight pieces on each side if it's summer, for the hours of daylight, at this latitude. Then see where the sun falls."

None of this was what Hillsinger wanted to say. He was not even sure it was true. He wanted to say, with Douglass, *It is easier to build strong children than to repair broken men.* He wanted Catta to know why this was happening to him, both tactically and in theory, and how it corresponded to desperate things that existed in the world. He wanted him to know the *Crito* in its entirety, the importance of coal production, all of Livy, certain passages in the *Federalist Papers*, and the tactical logic of subma-rines. *A child said what is the grass. Let the dead bury the dead.*

Hillsinger, whose training demanded that one must interro-gate oneself first, especially in moments of stress, realized that he was rambling, failing massively at what he could only imagine was an effort to rationalize the irrational parts of his thinking. He found himself clear in the basic decision, but unsure whether there should be some apparatus to it, some key to the experi-ence to tell Catta first. *How ridiculous*, Hillsinger thought—*if we are teaching endurance, then he does not need poetry.* Let Baffin be the teacher.

30

The *Heron* made the turn to starboard along the rim of the open sea, and Hillsinger could now see the outer islands of the archipelago. There was North Island with its two green hills, aberrations in the gray Atlantic. On the near side, the wastes of Pulpit and Sisters sat below North, and behind those two, with only its treetops now visible, lay the wilderness of Baffin. Sitting in the stern, Hillsinger turned toward Catta. He was committed: his logic was sound.

"Tell me what time it is," Hillsinger said.

Catta looked up, divided the sky, and counted.

"Four o'clock."

Hillsinger looked at his watch.

"It's just after three—note the position of the sun. You'll disembark at Baffin when we get there."

That's strange, Catta thought. *No one ever got off the boat at Baffin. Some kids held their breath when they passed, as if it were a graveyard.*

"Is the eagles' nest inland?" Catta said.

Cyrus had told him that no one ever walked past the tree line on Baffin, that the woods were too dense for walking or even picnicking. There were not even shellheaps, buildings, or any kind of ruins. *It's a wasteland*, Cyrus had said. He said the whole island was absolutely bad luck.

"James and your grandfather and I are going back to Seven," Hillsinger said, "and you will spend tonight on Baffin on your own."

"Would you repeat that, please?" Catta said.

"No."

There was no remarkable change in his father: his face and his expression were the same as always—thoughtful, curious, apparently serene. It was as if what he was saying was completely normal. That made Catta afraid.

His father had told him facts, figures, and history about a thousand places in the world, including most islands in the Seven archipelago—but never Baffin.

"We'll pick you up right here, right where we drop you off," his father said, "at exactly this time tomorrow afternoon."

"Why?" Catta said.

When their parents had parties on Avon Place in Georgetown, Catta and James were often led out into the living room to shake hands; James would leave immediately, but Catta would make himself small somewhere near his father, and listen to him talk in that definitive, lilting way about zinc or radar or inflation in Brazil (when his father said *inflation*, Catta thought of a hundred balloons all let go at once). For Catta, that tone was the only authentic seal of any statement's truth. And yet no one he knew had ever been past the Baffin beach. No one talked about it. The island was a void—a name without a body.

"What do I eat?" Catta said.

"You'll eat what you catch or find."

"What I find where?"

"The ocean is here," his father said, pointing to the ocean. "And the woods are there."

His father left him; he went up to the wheel and said something to Cyrus.

Catta saw four seagulls off the port side, although only two of them seemed to be traveling together. He wanted to stay on the boat. He wanted to circle these same islands on the *Heron* with this same configuration of wind and birds and this same light, at this same speed, until the end of time.

Now they were close. Baffin disappeared behind the North Island hills. Penny was up in the bow still, her ponytail exploding in all directions. Her pink shirt was dark; she was soaked and did not care. Unlike him, for her there was no moment when outrageous demands came due. Her day would unfold the way that days normally unfold on Seven or anywhere else. Light fades, the moon rises, day becomes night. The mind considers sleep. Penny would never believe what was happening here, just behind her.

They passed the small channel dividing North and Baffin, and then a pronounced headland. Soon Cyrus turned directly toward the beach.

"Are you ready?" his father said.

Hillsinger noted that Catta, when spoken to directly, did not look at him, nor at Cyrus or the Old Man or at James. He appeared to be studying the trees. Hillsinger smiled.

Let him be fierce, he thought.

Cyrus cut the motor and the *Heron* floated in silence toward the slope of Baffin's rocky beach. Catta could hear small waves underneath the hull, and then at last the crush of wet stones. He took off Cyrus's battered white hat and handed it back to him.

"You keep that," Cyrus said.

In the bow, Penny imagined that this was a group excursion and stood up to jump out onto the beach.

"Sit down," the Old Man said to her.

The Old Man, too, Catta thought.

Penny looked at Catta, perplexed, while James stood ominously behind her. Cyrus turned to Jim Hillsinger, who looked at his watch.

"Three seventeen P.M. Mark," Hillsinger said.

"Where are you going?" Penny said.

Catta climbed onto the foredeck and reached for the railing. He didn't say anything; he couldn't help her now.

James put his hand on Penny's shoulder to keep her from standing up, but she smacked it away. Then James put both hands on her shoulders.

Catta threw his shoes onto the beach, swung over the railing, and lowered himself into the cold shallow water.

"Let's go," his father said behind him.

"Too shallow for the motor here," Cyrus said. "We need a push back."

"Catta!" his father called.

Catta sat down on the beach and put on his shoes. He tied them slowly.

"James!" the Old Man said. "Get down and push us off."

James had been waiting for just that command. He jumped down and leaned his shoulder against the bow and slowly pushed the hull away from the beach. Cyrus lowered the outboard and then put the throttle into reverse. The boat shot backward, which pitched James over into the sea. Penny stood up.

"Wait," she said as the outboard started. "Catta's still there."

Catta turned, but he could not make out his father's expression. James was struggling to pull himself up onto the bow, where there was no ladder; his hand slipped and he fell back down.

"Stay there," Cyrus said, and he brought the boat around so that James, panting and soaked, could climb up the stern.

"Don't you see Catta?" Penny shouted again, now running back to the stern and pointing. Cyrus opened up the throttle and the boat shot forward, and then Catta could no longer hear what any of them said. Penny was screaming and the Old Man raised his arm to make some response, and then before long the *Heron* disappeared behind the trees of another headland.

31

As Lila and Isa walked home from the fairy houses, Sheila came out of the garden especially to meet them, or so it seemed to Lila. In the past, this girl, Cyrus's niece, had told Isa lovely things about what lambs ate or how to tell if a horse was asleep. She told them just yesterday about a nest of thrushes in the New House eaves. And yet, Lila did not at all intend to be friendly. Diana was a fabulist and a gossip, but it was still just possible that this girl had recklessly exposed Catta to—something. But what, exactly?

"Sheila!" Isa said. "We made a fairy house so big that squirrels and beetles can live in it, too!"

"Oooh," Sheila said, handing Isa a branch of rosemary from her pocket, "they'll like that. No one ever thinks of the squirrels."

That's true, Lila thought. *We do forget the squirrels.*

Lila smiled. On the spot, she chose to forgive Sheila for all of her womanly indiscretions, if that was what they were. This girl did not have any guile in her at all, and if anything she was too gentle for her own good. It might even show good judgment for Catta to have stirrings for such a plain girl who nevertheless thought of the squirrels.

"There were three lambs born in the barn," Sheila said.

Isa already knew this—Lila had told her—but Isa's appetite for hearing about the births was inexhaustible, and each time she heard it she was just as excited as the very first time.

Sheila knelt in the road and told Isa about the birth of the third little lamb, which she said was even now being nursed by

Betsy the Border collie. Isa had shrieked, and Lila laughed out loud.

"But what's his name?" Isa said sharply, although Lila had already told her at least fifty times.

Neither her mother nor Sheila could know the importance of this question. Neither of them could know that Isa suspected that things without names have hidden powers, which could be either good or evil, though never both. She stood there in the road, looking up at Sheila, hoping that this strange and wonderful lamb-dog still had a name because, if he did not, then she might have to be afraid of him.

"His name is Colt," Sheila said.

"That's a horse's name!" Isa shouted.

"It's a perfect name," Lila said. "May we visit him tomorrow?"

Lila thought a formal appointment was more solemn, more in keeping with the dignity of the event—three lambs! And all born just a hundred yards away, while they were here, on the island, and one of them nursed by a dog! Isa was in raptures. *When such a wonderful thing happens,* Lila thought, *one must do something more than just walk over to the barn and peer into a box. One must make a plan.* Happily, it also gave Isa something to look forward to that did not involve complex questions about the fairies.

32

Catta sat on the Baffin beach without moving. *This must be a joke*, he thought, *or a drill*. The *Heron* would turn around and come back for him. He watched the far edge of the headland and willed the boat to reappear. The pebbles in his hand were heavy. He had no matches, and fire was prohibited on the archipelago due to the drought. He had no food or water. Time had effectively stopped.

Cormorants were out over the ocean, but not those he had seen earlier. He picked up a small rock and tossed it into the water: he could easily have hit the boat's windshield, even after they had pushed back from the beach. He should have brought his emergency kit on the boat, the foil packet full of important things that he kept hidden in the Cottage basement. Why would he ever get on a boat without it?

Then Catta remembered the eagles—maybe he could find the eagles' nest that Edward Peck had seen. The nest must be big, he thought, and right on the tree line if it could be seen from the water. They said it was on the Seven side, so he started to walk that way. And then he stopped: *there was no nest*, he thought. *There are no eagles*. It had all been a trick to get him onto the boat with no explanation or argument. How had he not seen it? And yet, why would they bother? Here were three grown men conspiring—and for what? If any one of his father or the Old Man or Cyrus had said to go anywhere and do anything, he would have done it. He would not even have hesitated.

Catta walked back to where he'd come ashore and picked up Cyrus's old white hat from where he had thrown it. Not using his small handful of advantages would be stupid and prideful. Pride was what *they* had, what drove them to use what at other times his father called *strategies*. They had said the boat would come back for him tomorrow, but men who would lie about eagles would lie about anything.

The inside of Cyrus's hat had a patch that extended almost a quarter of the way around the band. It was made out of denim, and a corner of it was loose. That was what had been scratching him. Catta figured it was better to have a hole than to itch, so he tore off the patch. Something fell out onto the rocks. A thin tube of aluminum foil. He opened it and there were strange things inside—fishing line and a hook, two iodine tablets, matches, and an arrowhead. It was his emergency kit—or at least those parts of it that fit inside a denim patch on a battered old white hat. *What did it mean?*

It meant, he thought, that Cyrus had been with him all along. Martha, too—only she could have known about his hiding place in the Cottage basement. She could stitch a denim patch onto a narrow hatband, and then he remembered he had seen her walking back from the shop when Cyrus picked up the extra life jackets. Had that whole trip back to the dock been a way to get him this hat? And there was something even better: if Cyrus was with him—if not *everything* was a lie—then it was just possible that the eagles were real. He would look for them. Catta touched the point of the arrowhead with his finger, and it was sharp.

33

May 1960
Midtown, New York City

Hannah Quick went to the unmarked FBI office on three consecutive days. The friendly FBI man from two months ago, the one who had complimented her chicken, had come to their home again and "invited" her to have an informal conversation at their Midtown office. A few points of interest had come to light regarding Bobby Sheppard, he said, and she might be able to help. Billy had felt this was not an invitation she could refuse.

The conversation began cordially. The man, Agent Dent, called her "ma'am." He said he wanted to be transparent with her: he had information that she had been a member of the Communist Party in 1947. He said that this investigation was not about her, so there was no need for her to refute what he was saying, but did she remember seeing Bobby Sheppard at any of those early meetings? She did not. Then he asked many questions about the milieu of the Party in 1947, what the rooms looked like, how they communicated. He did not ask names, which surprised her, and which she would not have provided. Their talk was short and relatively painless, although he asked her to come back the next day. She came back. And then, midway through that second day, everything changed. A new man, Agent Harte, asked the questions now, and Agent Dent did not reappear. Now three silent men sat in the back of the room, occasionally grunting while Agent Harte interrogated her, bullied her, laughed at her.

You're a rich girl who got in over her head, he said. When did the Russians first contact you? Was it at a meeting?

I've never met a Russian, Hannah said. Most of the people at the Communist Party meetings were from the Midwest. For some reason, quite a few were from Minnesota. You are right, though, that I was in over my head, so I left. As I'm sure you know.

Hannah was made to envision herself in jail for perjury or treason, her children removed to foster care. Billy barred from his work. Their home and their assets seized.

There are two pillars of cooperation, Agent Harte said. The first is the absence of lying. So far, you have failed on that score. The second one is the presence of accurate information. It's true that you've given us some of that, although those are all things we already know.

My understanding, Hannah said, was that this was an informal conversation to provide background to your investigation.

Initially, that was true, Agent Harte said. But your evasions forced us to change our posture.

I am helping in every possible way, Hannah said. I am answering your questions when I know the answer.

Now they asked her names, and she declined. They threatened her. She was scared. She said she'd never seen Bobby Sheppard at any meetings, which was true, but they would not believe it. There were a lot of people at those Party meetings in those days, she said, and she knew very few people in Harlem at the time. It was possible he was there and she didn't know it.

Who is Hans Kallenbach? Agent Harte said.

I don't know, Hannah said.

Did you ever see Bobby Sheppard with Hans Kallenbach? he said.

I did not know Bobby Sheppard until much later, Hannah said. I met him at the school, a long time after I stopped attending meetings.

How many times did Hans Kallenbach come to your house? he said.

Zero times, she said.

Did Hans Kallenbach ever meet Bobby Sheppard at your house?

No.

This man's obsession with Hans Kallenbach told her that, for some reason, they wanted Billy. That she would never do. And when she refused, then what? Would they go after her daughters? Whoever and whatever else Hans Kallenbach was, he was now also a gun aimed at her family.

Agent Harte conferred with the other men who sat in the back of the room, and then returned to the table where Hannah sat with a small glass of water. Outside, it had started to rain.

Why don't I tell you about the old debutante balls? she said. Would you like to hear about the year they canceled Christmas?

Since our conversation has been unhelpful, Agent Harte said, we're going to stop this avenue of inquiry and refer the matter to the local District Attorney for criminal prosecution.

What is the charge? she said.

That's for him to decide, the man said.

As you wish, Hannah said.

It was here and now that the lightness she felt surprised her: something levitating, unsought, and unsponsored, a feeling in the register not of good fellowship and certainly not safety, but instead of comedy, the old comedies, as in the moment when all the mad chaotic strands suddenly meet and four couples are married at once by a disguised friar. The feeling was so unexpected that she laughed out loud.

I hope you understand, Agent Harte said, that the District Attorney is a very ambitious man.

Am I free to go? Hannah said. This was all already in the past, even this late twist, this obvious trick. She now felt, for the first time, that she had complete clarity around what was happening, and what to do.

We will recommend against criminal prosecution, Agent Harte said, if you give us an authenticated, complete list of your husband's investors.

Without his knowledge, said one of the men from the back of the room. *It was the first thing that man had said in two days.*

Yes, Agent Harte said. *That's an important point. Without his knowledge.*

Hannah could now see that they had been softening her up for this one request. The first questions from Agent Dent, the chicken-lover, had been designed to lower her guard, and then Agent Harte's role was to arrange matters so that she would always have the wrong answer, would feel beholden to their version of the truth. The idea, she supposed, was that after a while she would do anything to make amends, even betray her husband and her children.

I don't have access to that information, Hannah said.

Let me be explicit, Agent Harte said.

Yes, please, Hannah said.

Give us that list and we are done here, he said.

Thank you for taking such good care of me, Hannah said. *Shall I report here tomorrow? I think you said five days in total?*

Don't come back without that list, said the man from the back of the room.

Coming home, Billy's train stopped at Seventy-seventh Street and everyone had to exit. There were no cabs due to the rain, and he walked all the way home with a newspaper over his head. It was a Thursday, and the girls would be around the corner at their nanny's house. Inside, he found Hannah in the bath, which was no longer warm. She had opened two veins, one in each forearm, but what most people don't know is that veins will not do the job: it takes arteries. The inquest found nine distinct, smaller incisions before she hit an artery that would serve. Later, the coroner told him she had been dead for three hours by the time he arrived.

34

Billy Quick's girls were now at an age when they had more or less fully inhabited their names. When they were born, he had had no sense of what they ought to be called, only what they should be like, and it didn't occur to him that there might be a relationship between the two. He couldn't say how or why a name becomes immutable, but he was sure that with Ann and Barbara that final bonding was now done. They would never be Annie or Anna and Babs or Bee or anything else lyrical or cavalier: with such dull, middle-aged names he was afraid they were sentenced to a lifetime of sweaters and pearls. And so, weighed down by this lack of parental foresight, his girls frolicked, or rather attempted to frolic, on Seven Island's mile-long strip of white sand. They did not investigate, collect, capture, shout, or run. Instead, they played hopscotch, which they also did on the sidewalks of Central Park West. Billy blamed himself, although not too much, while he sat rummaging through his picnic basket.

Ann and *Barbara* had been meant to be placeholders, formal names from the Blackwells' formal family, and early on Hannah explicitly said that they would give the girls clever nicknames to balance out their stiffness. They put it off, though, and then they realized they disliked people who gave their children clever nicknames. Billy had pointed out the paradox of giving their children names from a family she had abandoned, and Hannah laughed and said she disagreed, that it was her parents and Lila and the others who had strayed from the true Blackwell path.

If the girls had more vivid syllables to live up to, Billy wondered, would they have jumped from the truck there and run screaming into the cold water like demons? Hannah had done that; in fact, that was the thing he saw in his mind's eye when other people used the word *grief*: he thought of Hannah running, especially into water, especially here on Seven. But these girls, *their* girls, Ann and Barbara, were controlled, careful, and precise: they liked tables and chairs, knew the names of fabrics. They were subtle, thoughtful, and endlessly appropriate. *Was it normal?*

Hannah had not been concerned. She had these blind spots of optimism; she saw the long-term as inevitably just, if you could live or see far enough into the future. She had trusted that Billy would understand, for example, without the maudlin summary of a note. The FBI refused all his inquiries, and when he pushed they went further and denied that she had ever been to their office. They had obviously threatened her and certainly him too, as a way to get to Kallenbach, and in retrospect, Billy thought, it had been just a matter of time before they connected Kallenbach to him. When they did, the FBI would have been convinced Hannah had lied, while she would have thought she was protecting him, protecting the girls. From time to time he had the thought that he had done this to her, which was some part of why Billy had chosen to tell the truth about the event itself. Lila had been his first call and had pleaded with him to invent something else. Anything else. She said, and kept saying, *think of the girls*, but from his perspective the only way to protect the girls, to keep the FBI away from all of them, was for the truth to be known. Was that not, in the end, the whole point? Was that not obviously what Hannah had wanted? What Kallenbach was involved in, he did not know. Clearly the man was being watched, so Billy could not take sudden steps in any direction—cutting off contact, refunding his money—without looking guilty, as if he were making a signal, which he was not. So he canceled their semiannual lunches at the Hungarian restaurant on Third Avenue. It was all he could do.

He looked down the beach and saw that the girls were now fencing with driftwood, a slight improvement. Behind them, a small pink blur emerged from the dunes and ran down the beach in the other direction.

"Penny!" he shouted, and the pink shirt froze.

Penny did not come any closer, or even move at all. Billy stood up and walked toward her, the girls trailing behind him.

Penny was breathing hard, her hands on her knees. She scanned the horizon over by Sisters Island. It seemed to Billy that she was trying to see around or over the headland and the islands. He had been too detached, he thought, too absorbed while Penny was here, but this was a chance to make amends: he had a basket full of food—salami, Seven Island cheese, tangerines. All children love tangerines.

"Come for a snack," Billy said. "We have tangerines."

Penny had thought there was a clear line of sight to Baffin from the Long Beach, but in fact a headland and two different islands blocked her view of Baffin. Fired by the shame of collaboration, she had leapt from the *Heron* even before the boat touched the dock. She ran the mile to this beach on the main dirt road. She had wanted to build a fire on the beach to signal Catta, and now, if she could escape her uncle, her plan was to cross the woods to find a spot with a clear line of sight to Baffin. She hoped she could see it from somewhere on the other side of that nearby headland, but if not, she would keep going until she figured out the winding geography of this place.

"Where are you going?" Billy said.

If she told him anything, Penny thought, she would lose time and the advantage of surprise. Adults were unpredictable, but she had to assume that her uncle was in league with the Hillsingers. She had to decide, here and now, whether to announce her defection from the tyrant's regime. It would be satisfying to make them all see her absolute defiance, though at the moment Billy seemed gentle and amused. It occurred to her that he might not know what had happened out on the *Heron*, so she chose to speak.

"Over there," Penny said.

"What's the rush?" Billy said.

"I want to see Baffin."

Behind her father, Ann rolled her eyes.

"Why?" Billy said.

"They put Catta there."

"What? How do you know?"

"I was on the boat and they made him get off."

Christ, Billy thought, *they actually did it.*

It was authentically bizarre that Hillsinger would do this thing, no matter how much it had been talked about over the years, and even stranger to have taken Penny with him when he did it.

"And when you see Baffin," Billy said, "what then?"

"I'll build a fire."

And then Penny looked at him with a sadness that was not a child's, and in that second Billy felt the heartbreak that had carried her here on such a clear day, on a dead run, wearing sandals, while his own lovely daughters jumped in and out of boxes drawn in the sand.

"I'll go with you," he said.

35

Jim Hillsinger was glad the Quick girl had run away from the houses. If he acted quickly, he could maintain some control over the narrative.

He and James were halfway up the ramp from the dock when he looked down and saw his father, still seated on the folding canvas stool by the wheel. His head was bowed, and he seemed absorbed in reverie or pain. The Old Man reacted badly if one drew attention to his occasional flights of weakness, so Hillsinger said nothing and kept walking.

"Go to the house," he said to James when they reached the top, "and find Aunt Diana. Ask her to show you something outside—ask her which flowers she saw in the chapel this morning."

"Why?" James said.

The truth was that Diana's presence would give the situation here a veneer of drama, which might keep Lila from seeing clearly.

"I need to speak to your mother alone."

At first, it was hard for James to stay calm when he saw that they were actually leaving Catta on Baffin. He was not used to feeling such waves of joy where his brother was concerned. Their father had not said what his crimes were, and—since James was himself guilty of a wide variety of undiscovered sins—he chose not to ask questions. Whatever it was, Catta deserved what he got. He routinely flouted James's rules for the Indian Game, which were always set by the oldest boy present. Catta was friendly with the staff girl Sheila and also with their pseudo-cousin Penny. He was a politician, not a soldier. By contrast, he, James, had expertly tied and untied the bowline and coiled it properly, as Cyrus had taught him. He had kept Penny Quick from standing up and causing trouble. He had pushed the boat off Baffin's beach and gotten soaked in the process, shivering in the wind all the way home. It was painful, but then the public shaming of his brother was fair payment.

But that one word from his father—that he *needed* to talk to his mother, alone—changed James's entire sense of the afternoon. If his mother did *not* know about Catta's punishment in advance, then it was not an official punishment after all. It was something else. He remembered now that spending a night on Baffin was something the Old Man talked about from time to time as if it were a *good* thing. What if everything James had done, all his vigilance and sacrifices, had contributed to the greater glory of his idiot brother? It raised the obscene possibility of the greatest possible horror: that Baffin had been, in some way James did not yet understand, not a punishment at all but a *gift*, just like so many other times when Catta did some ridiculous tap dance and everyone clapped. Still, he would do what was asked of him.

"I have to get a sweater," James said.

James crossed the rocks toward the Cottage, leaving his father behind.

36

Catta said a quasi-prayer for a massive haul of fish. He was not hungry yet, but soon he would be. He promised to eat everything he caught and leave the inedible parts for the cormorants, which Cyrus said were good luck.

He unwound the small coil of fishing line from his emergency kit, threaded the hook and tied it off, and then turned over rocks by the tree line until he found a night crawler. He speared it on the hook. Catta rolled the foil up, put it in the waistband of his shorts, and started out again along the island's circumference in the direction of Seven. Soon the rocky beach yielded to fields of kelp backing up to low cliffs. The kelp was so slippery that he had to take very small slow steps to keep from falling down. Off to his right the kelp crawled nearly halfway up a rock cliff, which meant that everything he was walking on now would be underwater at high tide, a small detail pointing to a serious fact: when the tide rose, this path would be cut off.

He came around the next headland and saw Seven in the distance. The channel separating the two islands was a fast-moving stretch of water three hundred yards across. Not so far, he thought, but Edward Peck said that underwater ledges created sharp changes in depth, which in turn made the currents dangerous; he said people had drowned there. Catta put out his line along a pool guarded by two large rocks, which together formed a shallow, protected area where water ran in and out with the small waves.

He looked at the forest behind him: it was almost impossibly dense. He wondered how the woods had come to grow like that—whether the soil or the climate was special or different here. He could see no point of entry at all. Were these woods dangerous? More dangerous than spending the night on the rocks, next to the ocean? He tied one end of his fishing line to a thorn bush by the tree line and let out enough slack to submerge the hook. He wrapped the line twice around a long stick to act as a floater. If he were a fish, Catta thought, he would like this pool. He decided to leave the line out here but keep moving and hope that, when he came back, a bluefish or snapper would be on the hook. He would clean it with his arrowhead and eat it raw.

A shade passed overhead and he looked up, hoping it was a cormorant—but no: just a gull. Behind the gull, though, across the channel, a thin line of smoke rose above the Seven treetops. He followed it down to its base on the shore by the waterline. Figures were close by, although too far away to say who they were. Something bright jumped up and then fell away again— they were building a fire. A pink blur darted out of the woods and onto the headland, and Catta laughed out loud. He saw Penny's hand in the air, and then he heard a shout. Other voices joined in after a delay. The wind and distance killed the words, but their intent came through. Catta answered back, gathering all his breath into a massive scream.

Catta turned away from the fire, and he felt something new rise up inside him, something decisive. *The ocean is here*, his father had said, *and the woods are there.* He had come from the ocean. He would go to the woods. He would cross Baffin on foot.

37

March 1964

Central Park West, New York City

The first time it happened was unexpected. Lila had come to New York to collect her nieces for the night, something she tried to do at least once a month in the immediate aftermath. It had taken Billy less than a month to vacate Hannah's dream of a Harlem counter-life, and he and the girls moved into a classic eight on the top floor of a formerly elegant building on Central Park West. By chance, the rooftop ballroom was empty and basically abandoned and Billy bought that too, since it lay directly above his apartment. He said one day he would build a staircase.

When the elevator opened at his apartment that night, Lila called for the girls but there was no response. The lights were all out, which was not terribly odd since the sun had just set. Lila went into the kitchen and opened the refrigerator door because she could not find the light switch. She laughed out loud—his refrigerator was empty except for mustard, champagne, and a fruit basket still in cellophane. Billy had come in silently, and turned on the light behind her. Lila was so startled that she dropped her scarf.

They're upstairs in the ballroom, Billy had said.

They both knelt to retrieve her scarf, and then his head was within a few inches of her exposed neck. Everything had just exploded. As a sexual experience, that time was unremarkable. As a form of insurgency or reconstruction, however, it was perfect. Afterward, Lila fetched her nieces from the old ballroom and they all laughed about their abject refrigerator.

It happened another time, and then again, each time with diminishing pretense. When she went up to New York, her friends all called her selfless and praised her devotion to her nieces. She began to remember what it had been like to be Lila.

It turned out that, over short periods, the clarity of Billy's pain had the power to turn Lila's former dislike into an erotic force. It had not been joyless, but then Lila was not in search of joy. Her own mourning was shallow, fleeting, intermittent, and after the initial shock, she told him, she forgot about Hannah for hours and even days at a time. She could not get closer to it. That distance made her very, very afraid.

Be glad, he said.

That, she said, would be monstrous.

You didn't love her, Billy said. You can't mourn a ghost.

Lila did not argue that day, which was March 18, nor did she announce or discuss. She reached for her compact. She took the girls to the Plaza one last time, where they ordered too much room service. From then on, the girls took the train to Washington instead of Lila coming to New York. She informed him of the new arrangement through his doorman. Jim disliked Billy, which made for a useful catharsis, and their common loathing had actually made their marriage stronger. At that point, it was not even lying.

38

Lila's afternoon was dismal. Billy's friends the Templetons were up from New York, and since Lila knew the wife's older sister from college, she invited them for tea while Jim was out with Catta on the boat. Catherine Templeton, however, was less charming than Lila remembered, and Christopher, the husband, defeated the wisdom of philosophers by seeming stupid without saying anything at all. To complete the farce, Diana invited herself to join them and then fell asleep in her chair. When all the tea was drunk, Jim came in looking windblown and asked Lila if she would like to take a walk over the hill. Lila had said yes, she absolutely would, and she would meet him on the lawn in thirty seconds—assuming that everyone present would take the hint. But the Templetons had lingered aggressively, and then Diana wanted to borrow a dress from Lila for the Migration dinner tonight. They tried several on, but nothing of hers would fit.

And then, at last, Lila was out in the open air again. Jim was waiting for her, and they walked away from the harbor, up over the hill to the back fields, where the landscape was earthier, greener, less obviously dramatic. Here, the beauty lay more in the everyday warmth of the farm: cows, fencing, bales of hay, a stone wall reaching deep into the woods. On this side of the hill, one no longer had the monumental sense of effortlessness. Some literalist had put bells on the cattle, and as the herd wandered into the trees, they sounded farther off than they really were, like a procession in a valley in the mountains. After a while, Jim stopped. Lila stopped beside him, and they stood together for a long time, looking at the sea.

"Tell me about Billy," Jim said.

He knew. In her mind, there was no doubt. She could deny, could answer literally; she could ignore the obvious depth of his question. All of it led to the same impasse.

"It was less than nothing," Lila said.

"Before or after Hannah died?"

"After. Because of."

"Were there others?"

"No. Never."

There was a pause, which lost its shape amid the evening sounds, the crickets and hidden frogs, and became a troubled silence.

"What now?"

"Nothing. It's done."

"And last night?"

"I didn't see Billy. I went to the chapel and then straight to Hannah's room."

For Lila there was no real secret here—no burden of hidden ecstasy. She was not in love with Billy.

"Someone saw you," he said. "Cyrus told me about it this morning."

"I don't know how."

If he were honest, Hillsinger thought, his own mistakes were equally bad. First and most dangerously, he had mishandled the Subotin affair. He had walked into Angleton's trap and then compounded the error by not telling Lila about it right away. They were both guilty of keeping the wrong secrets, but that was over now.

"I need some information," he said.

"Anything."

"Tell me about Hans Kallenbach."

Kallenbach! she thought. He wasn't even a footnote.

Lila described the two occasions in her life when she had spoken to Hans Kallenbach: at Billy's house, in passing, this past January, and then the evening not too long after that when Kallenbach called their home by accident. When she picked up the phone, Kallenbach had at first been confused, she said, and then he apologized, saying he'd meant to dial the number above theirs in his book. Including that exchange, she said, in her life she had spoken to the man for a total of less than five minutes.

"How did you know that I'd met him?" Lila said.

"Hans Kallenbach handles American money for the KGB. When he called our house you thought it was an ordinary wrong number, but in fact he was speaking directly to the FBI, who at the time was tapping our phone."

"Oh no," Lila said. "No no no."

"He was planting the seed with them that you and I were a husband-and-wife team spying on behalf of the Soviet Union. Somehow he knew the FBI was listening and he hoped they would flag the 'wrong number' as a coded communication— i.e., that some combination of his words was a prearranged cue for a meeting. Which they did."

"Why would Kallenbach do that?"

"At the CIA, there is absolute conviction that someone high-ranking is a traitor. The KGB knows this. If there is in fact a traitor, then accusing me and others protects them. If there isn't a traitor, then it creates confusion. Either way, they win."

"They can't have settled on you," Lila said.

"I'm on a short list."

"Even before Kallenbach called?"

"We will both be prosecuted if you repeat what I am about to tell you."

"I understand," Lila said.

"In March," Hillsinger said, "if you remember, I went to Virginia for the weekend. We had—we still have—two separate Russian defectors who disagree on important points. Their names are Astrakhov and Subotin. That trip to Virginia was what's called a Wise Men panel, and we were asked to choose between them—to say who was lying, and who was not. I said they were both telling the truth. I didn't know this at the time, but dangerous people internally had already decided that the second defector was a KGB plant—a provocation. Therefore, my view was automatically suspect."

"Is it grounds for prosecution?"

"Angleton was already investigating my role in Hannah's Board of Education situation in '55, which came to light only recently. His people see a clear pattern of aiding and abetting known Communists."

"Oh, Jim."

Lila could no longer hear the bells off in the woods. And the water was so still that she had not yet heard the bellbuoy.

"Can you tell me anything else about Kallenbach," Jim said. "Anything at all?"

"No."

"Take some time."

"No, I'm sure."

"Over the last six months," he said, "has any mail ever arrived opened?"

"No."

"Did any strangers approach you, in any capacity?"

"A vagrant told me that millions now living will never die."

"Anyone else?"

"It was odd that Kallenbach appeared at Billy's house when he did. He said he was passing by, but then he somehow had presents for Ann and Barbara."

"Would there have been any way he knew you were there?"

"I suppose it's possible Billy told him."

"Anything missing at home? Anything ever out of place?"

"No."

Hillsinger had already decided Lila's mistake was not nefarious. The simplest explanation also seemed like the right one: two grieving souls, an evolution of their purpose, some bad luck. If you went far enough back, Kallenbach was arguably Peregrine Wilkie's fault.

It was now obvious to him that Lila's affair was known to the KGB, and that her meeting with Kallenbach was not random. Kallenbach had guessed what was happening between Billy and Lila, or Billy told him, or KGB surveillance was in play. They saw in it a chance to turn Hillsinger or at least to sow confusion, since even without a mole the KGB would know that the level of tension at the CIA was elevated. The meeting was designed as a prelude to the "wrong number" phone call, so that Lila would sound on the (tapped) phone like she already knew Kallenbach. The FBI had duly recorded the exchange and forwarded it to the CIA. This one fact—that the KGB knew Jim Hillsinger was under active surveillance—was the clearest evidence Hillsinger had seen that there was a traitor at the senior level. If they had *not* known for sure, then having anyone call a CIA officer's house was a needless risk. The wrong number was a key link in the chain of events leading to Angleton accusing Hillsinger of treason, and yet if Hillsinger actually were a Russian asset, then the KGB would never have let Kallenbach call the house and bring down so much scrutiny. Therefore—in directing Kallenbach to make that call, the KGB themselves had exonerated him. *How had Angleton missed that?*

And where did all this leave Billy? Was he working with Kallenbach?

It seemed unlikely. Even allowing for Hannah's flirtation with the Communists, could he—could they all—have missed something that serious? And even if they had missed it, was Billy smart enough to manage a deception of that scale? Again, unlikely. By Hillsinger's reckoning, Billy was either a master tactician—there was no way—or he was Kallenbach's unwitting pawn.

"The children will adapt to New York," Lila said. "Everyone adapts."

Hillsinger paused.

"Catta's on Baffin for the night," he said. "We left him there this afternoon."

"You said never."

"The situation changed."

"How?"

"Are you seriously asking me that?"

"What did you tell him?" Lila said.

"That we'd be back at three seventeen P.M. tomorrow."

"That's it?"

"That's all he needs to know."

"Watch what I do."

"You won't do anything."

"If Cyrus or Edward Peck won't take me to Baffin, I'll find a canoe. I'll swim."

"If you go and get him," Hillsinger said, "or, really, if you are seen by him or anyone else as anything other than serenely confident in his ability to endure—then you will have created the worst of all possible worlds. You will not only have sent him to Baffin, but you will also have doubted that he could survive it."

39

Out on the headland, Billy Quick thought their bonfire could engulf the whole island if the wind picked up. Right now the sparks were blowing out to sea, but that could change. Penny ran back and forth between the woods and the tip of the headland, collecting more and more firewood, resembling more and more a frantic pink hummingbird. Ann and Barbara emerged from the forest, Barbara carrying rolls of birch bark and Ann a bundle of dry twigs.

He could not deny that the fire was reckless, but Billy told himself it was safer for him to help than for Penny to build it alone. He had initially hoped they would fail quickly and honorably and go home, but instead they had some limited success. The small kindling had caught right away. Then they built a cone of shorter logs above the first, now-smoldering pile, and then on top of that a lean-to of longer driftwood. It was an elegant structure, everything pointing upward. When the outer branches began to catch, Penny ran out on the headland there and shouted. It was Catta: they could just barely see him, a lighter shade against the trees. He yelled back and then they all shouted, Ann and Barbara too. It was nonsensical and wonderful. Defiance became hilarity, and then the girls slipped into mania. Penny ran everywhere, bouncing over rocks and stumps, carrying limbs higher than her head; Ann was laughing, as if unleashed from something; and Barbara fell down over and over again, from all the excitement. The three of them now circled a raging fire. Extinguishing it, Billy saw, would mean open revolt.

Soon enough the whole burning structure collapsed and the girls all shouted again, which for a moment stopped the parade of driftwood. For no apparent reason little Barbara said, "Ashes, ashes, all fall down!" and Ann laughed and screamed it too, and then Penny did, and they all chanted it together, laughing and shrieking. The fire was already huge, and Penny punctuated every "all fall down!" by throwing more and larger wood on it from the pile. *This*, he thought, *is how poetry destroys cities*. Some of the branches were so big that the girls had to lift all together just to raise them off the ground and heave them into the inferno. Anything lying nearby that was at all flammable was thrown into the fire, and Billy did not stop or even try to moderate them. Lila would say that overindulgence of his girls was one of his many failures, though he himself would call this a lesson in the contagion of happiness. He hoped to God the wind would keep on blowing out to sea.

40

Catta was five yards deep in the woods, and already he had cuts and scratches on most of his exposed skin. He had clearly miscalculated. Where he was now, close to the channel, was the easiest point of access to Baffin—it would be where every casual picnicker, trail-clearer, and day-tripper would land first and try to forge inland. Here, though, Baffin had defended itself: the trees stood close together, their branches all intertwined, as if the island itself were aware of its own vulnerability and had chosen to blockade the casual visitor. A more remote area might be more accessible. He should try the part of Baffin *least* likely to make for an easy landing, somewhere wind lashed, a headland facing the open sea, a place where even sailboats could not anchor. Baffin's northwest corner on the map opened onto the ocean. It was the slot between North and Sisters where a low, natural breakwater extended someway out into the sea.

To make it there before dark, he had a long distance to cover and not much time. Catta pushed into the woods every hundred yards or so to test them, and each time he was painfully turned back. His shirt was ripped; part of it was flapping. He could feel long welts on his back. If there was good news, it was that the tide was definitely headed out rather than in, lessening his chance of being cut off in the next few hours. His hands were sticky from breaking branches, and they smelled like sharp pine.

Last December, while walking on Wisconsin Avenue with his father, there was a line of Christmas trees for sale, and their smell had transported Catta back to Indian Head, as if it were some early morning in the summer. He was greedy. He plunged his head into the middle of them, and the whole row of trees fell down on top of him. The tree man was furious, shouting in a foreign language that turned out to be French. His father calmed down the startled man in his own language; Catta had not known his father spoke any foreign languages. In the end they bought three trees, and the man gave them one for free. One by one, they carried all four back to Avon Place, where they gave away the extras to their delighted neighbors. His father had said Catta should carry the top of each tree since that end was lighter, but instead he carried the trunk end so the sap would cover his hands. That night at dinner his fork kept sticking to his hands and his mother demanded to see them. They were black. She asked him to wash his hands. He refused. She insisted.

Catta was angry and embarrassed, but for some reason his reaction was much stronger than it should have been. He declared a hunger strike. He did not eat or leave his room all through the next day while James described all of his favorite foods in detail through his closed door. When his father got home, he came into Catta's room and sat quietly at the foot of his bed for what seemed like a long time. Finally, he said that the Constitution guarantees many freedoms, even for children, but that washing hands was not really much to protest. People on hunger strikes were often in jail, he said, and their friends and family were being killed in ways that would give him nightmares. The point was for Catta to know that these are serious things, done for serious reasons, and sometimes people died. Still, he said, the choice is yours. We will not force you to eat, though if you starve yourself now, what happens when something authentically important comes along? *Whatever decision you make*, his father had said, *will be the right one*. They had roast chicken for dinner that night, and it tasted better than anything Catta had ever eaten.

On Baffin, the light was failing. The night would be cool, especially by the water. Catta used the three waterproof matches left in his emergency kit to try to light a fire, but the needles and branches here were damp and wouldn't catch. He knew what hypothermia was, and now there was no hope of a fire. He had to pick an entry point to the woods and live with the consequences. If it was impossible to go more than five yards in, then he had failed: he would curl up at the waterline and suffer through the night. If all his theories were wrong and if on Baffin the penalty for being wrong was death, then he would find a rock to sit on, somewhere open to the sea, a place the *Heron* would easily spot his frozen corpse when they came looking for him. He would try to die upright like someone keeping watch, with a look of implacable scorn on his face.

Lila sat in a wooden chair at the small table in the kitchen, eating cornichons out of a jar. Nearby, Martha and Susan hovered over stovetops, chopping and sprinkling, producing the festive Migration dinner that Lila herself had planned months ago, via letters to Martha. They had called it A Dinner of Saints, from the recondite names of the main courses: Potage St. Germain and Lamb Kidneys St. Lawrence, both specialties of the Old Man's Boston club that Martha had adapted for the island.

"We need," Martha said to Susan, "four or five carrots from the garden for garnish."

"That's not on the sheet," Susan said. There was always a written *mise en place* for Martha's formal dinners hung on the wall in large print for the helpers. Lila wondered, briefly, if she had just eaten the garnish for tonight's dinner, which in fact she had.

"Go," Martha said, and Susan went.

Lila had, in her mind, no images of Baffin Island other than its long unbroken tree line that looked exactly like the long unbroken tree lines of a thousand other islands. She had only ever glanced at it from a boat. Catta would be cold, hungry, possibly wet. She imagined him shivering; he would believe or understand that, somehow, she too had done this to him. Her mother used to say the only thing she truly feared was the lucidity of her own children.

Lila was grateful for the sounds and smells of dinnertime, the clatter and warmth, a counterpoint to the accusation of everything else. These were the wages of sin: to sit in a warm kitchen awaiting a lovely dinner where she would be expected to soothe, flatter, and charm a set of guests, including Billy Quick, whose set of predatory indiscretions—exposing her to Kallenbach in January, apparently exposing her to Cyrus this morning, exposing her to God only knew who or what else— had now led them all into danger. *No*, Lila thought, *we have been lied to all along about sin. The true wages of sin are to have no options, to be forced to smile while the punishment is given.* Even if she chose to make an opera of her motherhood, to paddle a canoe to Baffin—then what? How would she find him? And if she did find him through some miracle, how would it seem to Catta? It would put him in an impossible position, forced to choose between parents, between competing ideas of order. She decided Jim was fundamentally right; there was nothing she could do. He had checkmated her, although she had made it easy for him. And now she had guests.

Martha asked if she should announce the soup, and Lila looked at the clock. How was it so late, so catastrophically late? The New House people would already be there—but who would welcome them? Diana? They would all be clumped in little groups, talking about the weather, while Diana Hillsinger lay down on the couch. Lila stood up. She had guests.

She crossed the kitchen just as Susan came back in, holding carrots pulled fresh from the garden. Tonight, Lila thought, there was something different about this girl. Susan was often distracted, even surly, but right now, despite the press of activity in the kitchen, she had an unusual stillness, even a glow—very much, Lila thought, like someone in love. And why not? She was pretty enough. Susan *should* have an admirer, or a lover, even—who knew what happened here once the families went to bed? In the last year alone, she knew of two untimely pregnancies among the staff.

"Mrs. Hillsinger," Martha said, "Do you mind if I give Mr. Quick rosemary instead of carrots for garnish? He don't like carrots."

"Of course, Martha," Lila said.

Martha had a natural tact, Lila thought, a delicacy that all the Park Avenue ladies could profit from. And then Lila deliberately said something that made no sense, since Billy's brother rarely came up and his father had been dead for years.

"Martha, we are talking about *Billy* Quick, aren't we? His brother isn't up?"

Susan's head had turned, ever so slightly, when Lila said his name. *It was him*, Lila thought—Billy Quick was Susan's phantom lover.

"Yes, Billy," Martha said. "He has three couples up with him now—Kipps, Templetons, Van Colls."

That he was irresponsible or opportunistic—that Billy abused his position on the island or *interfered with the staff*, as her mother would have said—was not at all surprising. If she had thought about it, she would have assumed as much.

"Of course!" Lila said to Martha. "You told me all of that just yesterday, didn't you?"

"Yes, ma'am."

And then her rage at Billy Quick brought about a minor clairvoyance—an answer to the riddle of how Cyrus had found her out last night. Lila pictured him roaming the New House late at night, finding her asleep on top of the covers in Hannah's room. He would have complimented himself on Lila's inability to stay away, and of course he had told someone—most likely Cyrus or one of the other staff, retailing it as an oddity, because he couldn't bear for it not to be known. And then, for obscure reasons of his own, Cyrus had told Jim. Otherwise, the coincidence of Jim's piecing so much together so quickly was too overwhelming. Was that also, she wondered, how it had worked with Kallenbach—was that why he showed up, with presents, on the exact day she visited? Billy had simply been unable to control himself.

She opened the swinging door that led to the butler's pantry, and then the outer rooms.

"Thank you, Martha," Lila said.

"For what, Mrs. Hillsinger?"

The wind rose as Catta approached the open sea. If he had been a bird, or if Sisters Island were not blocking the view to his left, then he could have seen the Long Beach on Seven while he walked. North Island was up ahead, around a few more headlands. Spain lay somewhere in that direction, too, across the ocean. The seaweed was slick; he had to take little steps. He was sure that this time he would break through, into the Baffin interior. Catta turned and walked inland yet again.

He was immediately pinned in place, stopped by a wall of branches five yards past the tree line, with one leg draped over a low limb and his front arm against what seemed like holly bushes grown into the shape of a net. He was stabbed from every direction, somehow everything here had spikes on it. With immense difficulty, he backed out the way he had come in.

He knelt down by the ocean and rubbed salt water on the scratches covering his arms and legs and torso. The dusk was long this time of year and there was enough light left to try one more new entry point farther around the island. *Choose well*, he told himself, *because the next one is where you suffer and do not stop.*

He walked along the island's rocky apron for a longer stretch, and across from him were Sisters and Pulpit and their interlocking coves and shallows that were so dangerous that even Cyrus would not drive a boat here unless the Old Man directly ordered it. The birds were more curious, as if they were not used to seeing people. He saw three cormorants again, which he took to be good luck. Soon the impatient ocean lay once again in front of him, in a narrow window between the Pulpit and North headlands. This was where he had imagined the forest would be more forgiving, where like the inquisitive birds he hoped that isolation had made the woods less guarded. That was his theory—his intuition. What was definitely true was that so far every intuition had been wrong. What if he was blocked and pinned again? What if he lost his bearings? What if, even in twilight, the forest was too dense to see the water, and he had no sense of where he was at all? Was Baffin big enough to go around in circles forever, or at least until he starved? He ate some seaweed. It was full of rancid little bubbles. It tasted awful. Aunt Diana said that seaweed had good nutrients, that you could live on it. His father had laughed at her.

Now Catta lay down on the rocks and closed his eyes. He fell asleep for a short time, and when he looked up at the sky again, it was completely dark. He saw Big Bear and the Big Dipper and tried to fix their positions in his mind so he could navigate by them, even roughly, just to know where the ocean was. He rinsed his mouth with salt water to replace the grim taste of the seaweed, and then he split off a limb from a pine tree by the water. He rubbed the pine pitch from the branch on his hands and arms and legs and all over his face. He picked up a piece of driftwood and threw it at the wall of branches. Now he was ready.

43

January 1964
Central Park West, New York City

*Sometimes they went to the unheated ballroom on the roof. His aviary,
Billy called it, from the endless pigeons on the ledge. There were blankets
and a thrift shop chair and sofa, concessions to his daughters' tea parties.
It was enough.*

How are you? Billy said, afterward.

I'm bored with you, Lila said.

She could feel him smiling in the half-light.

The girls must be ready, he said.

I'll collect myself.

Lila opened her compact with a click, *and a thousand pigeons rose
up in a body, as if in answer to a prayer.*

Billy said something and then left, and the word downstairs *formed
an echo among the high windows. It had surprised her, how efficient the
absence of pleasantries could be.*

*When Lila arrived in the kitchen, Billy was sitting at the table
with a man she did not know. She was alarmed. He was older, gray,
most likely in his late fifties, elegantly if casually dressed. He spoke
idiomatic English with a strong accent. Billy introduced him as Hans
Kallenbach.*

Are you Austrian, Mr. Kallenbach? Lila said.

*No, thank God, Kallenbach said, smiling. Why would you say such
a thing?*

Your shoes, Lila said.

He wore exquisite burgundy loafers that no American shop would ever have stocked.

You're teasing me, Kallenbach said. The Austrians dress like peasants.

Lila smiled. She was intensely aware of Billy watching her.

Excuse me, she said. I'm here for my nieces.

Had Billy known this man was coming over? she wondered. Was he that stupid, or that reckless?

Lila went into the back bedrooms, where the girls had not begun to pack for their overnight at the Plaza. Within minutes, Lila had pajamas and nightgowns and teddy bears and toothbrushes arranged in two tiny suitcases. The packing and unpacking, Lila thought, were arguably the most important parts of her visits.

Back in the kitchen, Kallenbach had placed wrapped presents for the girls on the table. They were delighted—an unknown man who brought presents! Inside the boxes were beautiful French-style scarves. Ann and Barbara said thank you very gracefully, despite their total confusion at the meaning of these squares of patterned silk. Lila thought that Hans Kallenbach must be in the habit of giving presents to girls somewhat older than six and eight.

Put them in your suitcases, Lila said to the girls. We'll have a scarf-tying lesson at the hotel.

Billy says you live in Washington, Kallenbach said.

I'm afraid so, Lila said.

It's a miserable city, Kallenbach said.

It's much too hot, Lila said, although the cherry blossoms are lovely. That was a joke she had with Jim.

Billy says you know the good Ethiopian restaurants.

What an odd thing for Billy to tell anyone, Lila thought.

It was perfectly true—they often went to a particular Ethiopian place with the children, who liked to eat with their hands. Kallenbach said he would call her for a recommendation when he next came to town. He seemed very comfortable asking people for favors. When she left with the girls fifteen minutes later, he and Billy were drinking coffee at Billy's kitchen table.

44

Diana Hillsinger stood in the living room, surrounded by faces, and she knew that her first instinct was right. She should have stayed in her room.

At her own parties, Lila was first to arrive and the last to leave, but tonight she had not appeared. It was very strange. Lila was not in the house or on the lawn or even in the chapel, and now she was missing from the living room. The handful of people already dressed and present, some of them strangers, presumably New House guests, were standing in scattered pairs, more or less balkanized, which Lila would hate. John Wilkie was in the corner by himself, nodding apologetically. It was all too much.

Diana was about to retreat back upstairs when her eyes found the desperately ugly ceramic owl that she herself had insisted they keep in the living room. Now the owl reproached her. Her premonition had been right—the catastrophe had come to pass. This was her moment. If Lila were somehow incapacitated, and if what James related to her was actually true—that Catta was out on Baffin for the night—then Diana would give everything. She would play the hostess, or at least attempt it. She would become one of those women whom she routinely mocked for their hypocrisy and their sweaters. She could endure anything for ten minutes.

Diana plunged into the living room with abandon. She asked Catherine Templeton about her horrific shoes and then dragged her over to Wilkie, who could be shy among strangers, but who,

Diana had learned, knew Catherine's brother-in-law from summer camp. She recruited the outrageously stoic Christopher Templeton to mix martinis, and in the process discovered two things, both wonderful: one, that the poor man was desperate to be useful, and, two, that conversation in that area exploded when he left. She complimented the Van Colls and the Kipps, more of Billy's guests, on their combined total of eight lovely boys, who were without exception appalling barbarians, even the little ones. As a precaution she introduced her own guests, the Petersons, to everyone in the room several times over, since they had a tendency to get drunk. In Diana's experience, it was only the unknown drunks that anyone objects to. She took the tray from Susan, and through the medium of toast points smeared with goose liver, tried to bring to this room that fluidity, that lightness of spirit that was the hallmark of all of Lila's parties and the opposite of how Diana herself had felt since lunchtime today, when she had had her premonition.

Jim Hillsinger arrived downstairs later than he had hoped, and he was surprised to be offered foie gras on a silver tray by a lively and attractive woman bearing an uncanny resemblance to his sister.

"These birds died in your service," Diana said to him.

Hillsinger had forgotten that Diana was capable of this sort of thing, although she killed the effect by saying *honk* as she passed onward. The serving girl, who was passing beef with horseradish, leaned close to him and whispered that the Old Man had rung the bell several times for chicken broth. Trays were to be left outside the door, and otherwise he was not to be disturbed. It was concerning, given his father's state when they returned from Baffin. Hillsinger asked Susan to keep him informed.

When she entered from the kitchen, Lila was shocked to hear a room come extravagantly to life. Diana ran across the room and embraced her.

"I'm completely adrift," Diana said.

45

Catta had been wrong again—the trees were *not* less dense opposite the sea. Sharp spikes dug into him from all sides. He could see nothing. All of his strategies had failed. Somewhere above him were the stars, but the woods here were completely dark.

So he went slack, disengaged his arms and legs, even his neck. Catta fell, landed on a sharp branch, and cried out. He took a few seconds to recover and then reached forward in the dirt, expecting to find a wall of limbs—but no: the lower ground was clear. There was space ahead of him if he stayed very low. He crawled forward under branches and around trunks and over hard roots until he was stopped again by a set of wide trees whose roots and branches forced him sideways. That was dangerous. He risked going around in small circles on Baffin, forever.

Are there bears on Seven? he wondered. *Scorpions? Warthogs? Malaria?* He tried to scare himself and called up all the bogeymen he could think of. *Copperheads?* No—none of those, definitely not—although the other day his mother had seen a green snake on the harbor trail, and she screamed. In a museum, Catta had seen a painting of an eagle with a snake in its talons, and he wondered if there were really eagles on Baffin, and—if they were here—would they fight bears and snakes? The painting argued that they would, but they had lied to him about the eagles once already. Or had they? *Was the eagles' nest a lie or not?*

He slid forward on his stomach, and when that was blocked he stood up and took half-steps to one side and lowered himself down again, through the spikes. He paid for every inch of progress. Feeling a void at head height above him, Catta threw a leg up and onto a higher branch and climbed over, landing carefully, avoiding the sharp leaves. He no longer had any real bearings, not the Big Dipper or anything else. His only reference was some faint intuition of a downward slope: the Old Man had told him once that an area toward the center of Baffin was below sea level in a sort of ravine, which explained some unusual plants and animals there. Therefore, downhill meant inland, until he reached the lowest point. *But if no one ever came here, then how did the Old Man know that?*

Catta was cold when he stopped moving and hungry when he thought about it, although the Baffin interior was protected from the wind and therefore somewhat warmer than the shore. This, he thought, was how the world crushes you. There was no announcement. No freakish blow or lightning or floods or even bears. No mystery, not even any struggle or surprise. It was fantastically simple. You were forced into a series of small bad decisions that slowly and irrevocably cut off your options. And then, once you were confused and desperate and worn down by hunger and cold and whatever else—when at last you could no longer move or think—then the crows came down from their trees.

Suddenly—shockingly—he walked three steps in the clear, and his movement chased away despair. His approach to darkness changed. *Take three steps*, he thought, *and then start over.*

If he could forget the cold for thirty seconds, then he would lie down. If he took *four* steps forward in a row, then he would call it a clearing; if there was a clearing in the woods, then he would lie down, and he would sleep. If that was impossible, then the second he felt the gentler touch of a pine tree anywhere on his body—if he could break off a needle and smell fresh pine pitch—then he would lie down at the base of that tree. Then he would sleep. You are still OK on food and water, so now find sleep. Then keep moving. If he followed these simple steps, Catta thought, the crows would stay in their watching trees.

He reached out five times, and there was nothing. On the sixth he felt the soft fingers of a pine tree in front of him. He broke off a small branch and inhaled the pitch. Now he could sleep. He lay down on the ground and wrapped himself around the trunk, with his head on one arm. He was covered with rough needles and dirt, and the tree's lowest branches rested on his shoulder. He wondered if he could sleep this way, or any way at all. He wondered if sleep on Baffin was the same as sleep in other places.

46

Lila watched Billy Quick eat from across the table. In all the years she had known him, through the shapes and mazes of their acquaintance, she had never noticed that he ate in these preposterous short bursts. Infinitely precise about cutting and arranging his food, Billy would stop and lay down his knife and fork, exactly parallel, tips at the center of the plate, and then talk in one direction or the other with violent hands, like a cartoon, before raising his fork again and spearing a loose pea and taking a bite from one of his separate piles. Then he would place knife and fork down, again very correctly, with the same practiced motion. It was so absurd that she almost laughed out loud.

As she watched him, the serving girl raised the half-finished plate from Billy's right side—and *there it was*. Susan's eyes flickered over Billy for just half a second too long. The effect was subtle, not more than a tremor. With an armful of plates, though, the extra half-second unbalanced her, and she had to touch the back of Billy's chair with her free hand. She was searching— taking risks to learn her fate. Only Lila had seen her, and only Lila could have formed these scattered bits into a picture of the truth.

Billy had fallen for Hannah very early on. Lila remembered the night as beautiful—right when the War started, just after the *Messiah* performance at the church. That felt like the end of something—it *was* the end of something—and everyone stood outside for hours in the falling snow. It was a moment in time when even nonexistent love could easily have been invented. He and Hannah had only met in passing—Lila had introduced them—but eventually the crowd pulled them all in different directions, and then when the War was truly underway, Billy's family had moved briefly to London, but when he came back, he had not forgotten her. Within a month, he knew Hannah's last name, where she went to school, and, crucially, her usual route home. He never revealed the sources of this information.

He saw her pass several times (he had told Hannah) but never stopped her. He was playing a different and much longer game than mere acquaintance. After school, Billy installed himself at a faded coffee shop about halfway between their home and Hannah's school. He sat in the window of Café Aurelian every afternoon, smoking elegantly—the way he smoked was always his best trick—glancing at newspapers, entertaining friends, knowing the names and histories of the café's amused Austrian waiters, whom he spoke to in tourist German. All of it to camouflage the fact that he was waiting for Hannah to pass by.

At first, Billy had not said or done anything at all: he was merely *there*, every day after school. Hannah told Lila that Billy would look up, lazily, always in another direction than outside, seemingly absorbed in the hieroglyphs of his cigarette smoke. The point, however, was that she did notice him. She learned later that his whole day built up to that one moment of choosing *not* to look at her, and deciding how best to do it. To preserve an element of randomness, he would ask a waiter for the dice cup and pick two numbers, say eight and three. If they came up, he would not look up at all when he felt her pass, which he described as an outrageous feat of asceticism. If his numbers *did* come up, then he would look up halfway, just enough to see her in the corner of his eye, but not enough to meet her glance if she should turn. He could tell from blocks away when she was coming, he said. He said he could *feel* it when she had turned the corner onto Lexington Avenue. When she would actually walk by, when she was right next to him with only a thin pane of glass separating them, Billy told Hannah it was like a wave breaking over him in the ocean. It might have been true, but then again Billy was a fantastic liar.

The shadow play went on for months. Every day Hannah walked by the window, and every day Billy was there in her peripheral vision. She looked straight ahead, and so did he. And then he vanished. Hannah noticed—she wondered about his health. *Was he smoking too much?* In fact, Billy had been legitimately sick for a few days, but then he stayed away out of despair, thinking he'd somehow lost his chance, squandering the mystery built up over such a long time. Only later did he see absence as a tactic. After a week, Hannah walked inside the Aurelian and drank a citron pressé at Billy's usual table to gauge how far down the street he was able to see her. She was too shy to ask the waiters about him. Once three weeks had passed, she'd almost forgotten that slight pressure of expectation that came when she turned the corner onto the otherwise barren stretch of Lexington Avenue. The Aurelian's window had lost its mystery and glamor, and that storefront had retreated, once again, into normal oblivion. And then he came back.

One day passing the window, Hannah looked up out of habit, almost as a reflex, and there he was—staring back at her. She lost all composure, broke off her gaze, and almost ran. That was when Lila first heard about the boy in the window of Café Aurelian. By making eye contact, Hannah had forced herself to admit that she was not indifferent to his presence. Billy was once again there every day, but neither of them looked up again. That first moment of contact had opened a wound that took a period of willful blindness to heal. Finally, passing by one especially cold February day, Hannah looked away until it was almost too late—and then she looked up at the window. What happened next was controversial: Hannah said Billy waved, but Billy said he simply gestured with his cigarette, at someone else. Hannah had waved back. It was a good-natured argument—who'd initiated that crucial wave and set history in motion. Whether Billy had risked everything to make contact, or if (as Billy claimed) it was Hannah who made the leap while he was merely asking for more coffee. Either way, Billy said, at that point there was no doubt. Conversation, love, marriage, children's names—they were all, he said later, implied in that first unspoken exchange, as the acorn implies an oak.

Lila wondered how it would have started with the serving girl. Despite the immense woods and open spaces on the island, it was not easy to run off alone here. Billy bent down to pick up something from the floor—his napkin—while continuing to talk to Christopher Templeton, two people over from him. Something flashed in Billy's other hand—*what was it?* He was twirling a silver butter knife through his fingers, like a drum majorette's baton.

"Jim, does your father refuse to join our community of saints?" John Wilkie said from the other end of the table, possibly drunk, Lila thought, and somewhat louder than the noise of conversation.

That anodyne question silenced everyone. The Old Man had not come down, which was unusual. He loved ceremonial occasions.

"He sends his regards," Jim said to the assembled company, as everyone had turned toward him. "The man was not born a sailor."

"To his better health, then," Wilkie said, lifting his glass.

"Hear, hear," Christopher Templeton said, also too loudly.

"Thank you, John," Lila said. "I know Mr. Hillsinger would agree with me when I say that all anyone needs to be made whole is one night under these roofs, in these beds, in front of these fires. May the Old Man and Seven Island live forever."

"Hear, hear, goddammit!" Christopher Templeton shouted, now banging on the table. He was agreeing with her, but Lila liked his silence better. She smiled her famous smile—the same one, Wilkie thought, that had brought at least three men he knew to the brink of suicide.

Wilkie raised his glass. He sensed the subterranean reproach in Lila's toast—she didn't like it when one conversation dominated a table—but just now he had other things to think about. He was absorbed by Lila's silent focus on Billy Quick throughout the entire dinner.

For his part, Billy Quick was happy: it was unusual and surprisingly festive for the New House to be invited over. This formal sort of thing was what the Hill House did best. The only awkward piece was Susan the serving girl, who had thrown herself at him behind the barn two nights before. It made for an interesting evening in the open air, although he had probably talked more than was wise. She was not impressed by the details of his mourning.

And then there was Lila. She had stared at him persistently through the whole evening; he wondered if she'd discovered he was avoiding the food, which was terrible. Meanwhile, his unfortunate houseguest Christopher Templeton was drunk and talking too much, and Billy was sure Lila objected to him, too. It was fair enough, but he wanted to catch her at it. He wanted to make her ashamed, but he kept missing his chance. Lila was too crafty, or too fast. Once he thought he had her, but instead she was cheerfully outlining, to Catherine Templeton, the pageantry of tomorrow's Migration. All of it, Lila said, had been invented from nothing by the Old Man.

47

Catta did not so much sleep there at the base of the pine tree as skate above a black sheet of ice made out of sleep. His dreams were literal, redundant, dry postponements of his waking— *Catta sleeps at the base of a pine tree* or *Catta's eyes open and see nothing.* Not dreams: reportage. He was nevertheless aware, in his half-sleep, of being unable to smell anything. Someday, he thought, he would like to have a dream made up only of smells: biscuits, pine pitch, grass, salt, smoke. And then he dreamt of fire. Torches suspended in the air grew larger, moved closer, and then, from nothing, spoke in meter and rhyme. *No*—they didn't speak—he was dreaming a song he already knew. Other voices joined the chorus—*It's a long way . . . to Tipperary!* He woke up, and, now awake, he saw that his dream fire was actually flashlights.

Three voices carried the song. They passed by twenty yards from Catta's head and moved away much faster than he would have thought possible, given the thickness of the trees and scrub. *There must be a path*, he thought. He could not turn to follow them—the dry brush rustled even when he breathed—but only one voice sang the verses, so Catta turned and stood up when all three sang the chorus. Then all at once the singing stopped and the lights vanished, as if they were swallowed up by the earth.

After a few moments, Catta moved carefully in their same direction of travel, slithering and sometimes tracking back to go around obstacles, pausing often to listen. At this distance, even if the singers heard him, they would think he was an animal. On Seven, the trails were lower than the surrounding forest floor, so as he walked he dragged one foot lightly behind him, feeling for a difference in grade that might indicate a trail. In front of him a glow emerged, a short arc or a notch, and he began to think he was looking down a sort of chute that passed between two larger bulks, possibly boulders. The Old Man had said there was a ravine. *What if,* he wondered, *I went over a cliff in the dark? How far would I fall?* The ground dropped slightly and he lost his balance—he fell—though not onto the leaves and scrubs he had expected, but onto hard-packed, rocky dirt. Feeling the ground, the hardpack was less than a foot across and extended farther than he could reach in two directions. This was the path. It might be a dry gully, he thought, or maybe a small creek, when there was no drought.

The faint glow increased as Catta moved closer. Now he could hear work sounds: shouting, metal on metal, thuds. He tried to climb the left-hand boulder, but it was mossy and his foot slipped. His left arm hit a low-hanging branch. The leaves rattled.

"What's that?" a sharp voice said below.

"Ghosts," said another voice.

"All the ghosts are on North," said a third voice.

There was a long pause, and Catta thought he heard foot-steps. Without thinking, he made an owl sound.

Hoot.

There was another pause. Down in the ravine, he could feel the men listening.

Hoot, hoot.

"It's an owl," said the first one.

The staccato work began again. Catta found good footing and climbed until he could see down into a small depression with steep sides. Was it possible this was the Old Man's ravine? At the bottom a single lantern gave very pale light, and he saw a machine with long tubes and coils and glass reservoirs. The three men moved large jugs to a spout at one end. The sarcastic voice that had said *ghosts*, the one who seemed to be the leader, opened up a wax paper package and took out half a sandwich.

Catta was fantastically hungry.

48

March 1964
Camp Peary, Virginia

Jim Hillsinger had woken up early and driven nearly three hours to southern Virginia to arrive at dangerous ground.

Good morning, Mr. Hillsinger, the functionary said when he checked in. You're in Room Two.

The CIA Director had summoned him that Wednesday and made an unusual request. Would Hillsinger go to the Farm on Friday to take a look at a defector? It's a Wise Men panel, the Director had said. Block out the weekend.

The Farm was the CIA training facility at Camp Peary; Wise Men panels were internal tribunals whose stated purpose was to give the Director disinterested, third-party assessments of controversial questions. If a question or issue could not be resolved inside a given department, or if it was so high-profile that broad consensus was necessary for political cover, then at least three senior staff from uninvolved departments were brought in to examine the case from the start. The stakes were high: when a panel's decision was unanimous, the Director adopted it. The meetings were famously contentious.

Room Two was a windowless space with a small desk. On it Hillsinger found a manila folder that, ominously, had a yellow sticker on its tab—the insignia of Counterintelligence. It was unusual for that particular department to ask for outside opinions, or for that matter to share their files. In theory, Counterintelligence was the agency element responsible for detecting KGB penetrations into the CIA. The head of it was James Angleton. At a very young age, Angleton had had major successes in the old OSS in Italy during the war, and he was considered a prodigy; at the CIA, he became a legend. Angleton approved all defectors, and since one cannot speak about foreign defectors without also speaking about traitors at home, Counterintelligence had also become, in practice, the secret police of the CIA.

The folder on the desk in Room Two held a stack of memoranda from Angleton's staff, summarizing the take from a KGB operative named Astrakhov. He had defected three summers ago; everyone knew about him, though before today only a lucky few had seen the actual documents. Most surprising to Hillsinger were the specifics in the material—well-sourced facts of the kind that made careers domestically and, if discovered, got agents killed overseas. Missile counts, arming protocols, long-range troop projections. Red Army contingency plans for Berlin in case of a ground war. This level of information was never shared, and certainly not by Counterintelligence.

Angleton was said to rely heavily on Astrakhov for his view of the motives, procedures, and operational capabilities of the KGB, which in turn suggested that Astrakhov's transcripts were the blueprint for the Counterintelligence view of the world. That being true, Hillsinger could not work out what Angleton was aiming for by sharing all this—was there doubt about Astrakhov's status?

Now what? Hillsinger said to the functionary outside Room Two when he was through reading.

I've been instructed to ask you, the functionary said, if you are now sufficiently familiar with the prepared material.

Yes, Hillsinger said. Sufficiently.

Hillsinger followed him outside and then into a room in another building. In that room were three CIA men: an older man from the Far East division named Danziger, whom Hillsinger knew slightly and did not like; Cressie, a junior member of Angleton's Counterintelligence

*team, whom he knew only by sight; and then Raymond Todd, someone
he didn't know at all, from the Office of Security. They shook hands in
silence. As a group they were not natural colleagues, the working concept
of the Wise Men panel being to bring together divergent points of view.*

*Cressie, the Counterintelligence man, called the meeting to order
despite being by far the most junior person in the room. That confirmed
this as Angleton's show.*

*We have a newer asset, Cressie said. There has been some contro-
versy as to whether or not we accept him as a legitimate defector, and, at
the suggestion of the Director, we are opening up this assessment to the
collective mind. We are grateful that you all were able to come down here
to help.*

*Cressie was obviously lying. Counterintelligence did not socialize
their decisions. In Angleton's view, no one's security was tight enough,
no one's loyalty far enough beyond question, and everyone else's historical view of the Soviet problem was superficial. Something else, Hillsinger
thought, was happening here. The problem, however, was that, with the
Director involved, he would have to play the whole thing relatively
straight.*

*Between now and Sunday, Cressie continued, you will witness a
limited debrief of Felix Subotin, an unratified defector out of the KGB's
Second Directorate. While Subotin first made contact with us in Geneva
in 1962, he was not brought to the States until very recently. Much of
his narrative is in conflict with the Astrakhov material you have just
read. Your task, Cressie said, is to decide which man is lying.*

*Hillsinger knew that when Subotin first contacted the CIA station
in Geneva, there was uncontained excitement. The cables from the field
officers, normally so terse, used words like* unprecedented *and* break-
through. *Subotin's father was a decorated hero of the Red Army who
later served as Stalin's shipping minister, and the son claimed to have
worked in a particular branch of the KGB that had never before produced*

166

a defector. Hillsinger himself had been asked by Angleton to consult on a minor angle touching Poland, Hillsinger's area of particular expertise.

Cressie led the three men out of the room, out of the building, off the paved walkways, and into the woods. They walked down a winding, freshly-cut path, and soon arrived at a cleared spot in the woods with a large cabin. Two armed guards patrolled the perimeter.

As you see, Cressie said, we have built a dedicated facility for debriefing Felix Subotin.

Inside the large cabin was a small living room where two officers were playing cards—the on-premise security. Cressie led the group to a room with a one-way mirror and a bare interrogation setup on the other side. As of yet, that room was empty. He did not know anything about the hydraulics of Subotin's emigration, but the building of a personal prison would suggest that things had gone wrong somewhere.

This is the debriefing room, Cressie said, unnecessarily.

Hillsinger did not talk to the others. He was sure everything on both sides of the glass was being recorded, and he assumed, too, that the three of them were chosen at least in part because they had no preexisting relationship. In that context, friendliness would read as a lack of objectivity.

On the other side of the glass, a man entered whom Hillsinger recognized as Miles Harris, Cressie's direct superior at Counterintelligence. Harris was followed by the two security officers from the living room, each of them holding one arm of a handcuffed man who seemed unable to walk properly. The struggling handcuffed man was Felix Subotin. He looked like he hadn't slept for days. To Hillsinger's knowledge, what was happening here was almost unheard-of—a hostile, possibly even violent interrogation on U.S. soil, with a willing defector no less. The security officers removed Subotin's handcuffs and placed him in a seat at the table. Harris passed Subotin a pack of cigarettes and a lighter.

Now you give me cigarettes? Subotin said.

Certainly, Harris said.

Why? Subotin said. Now you have important guys here behind glass? Is that why cigarettes now? Who is here?

Just you and me, Harris said.

Subotin then turned to face the one-way glass.

They try to kill me, Subotin said. Now you know.

49

The living room fire was burnt down to stubs in corners, but it still gave good light. Billy saw that everyone was arranged so a little taste of the fire fell on some patch of skin, just enough to hold them until the sun came up again.

There was no liquor he wanted and it was too early for bed, so he decided to rebuild the fire. He was of course aware that fires on Seven were a source of proprietary feeling—the Old Man was more vigilant about the fireplaces than his money—but then the Old Man had not come down tonight. *Fires and animals*, Billy thought, *belong to whoever takes care of them.*

His route took him by John Wilkie's left shoulder, which he tapped in passing. Wilkie nodded in return. The magnificent dinner had left John Wilkie feeling that the world was fundamentally as it should be. For example, it was difficult to cook lamb kidneys properly, but Martha had done it—and then there was the theater of the whole thing. Diana's remarkable performance during cocktails, the dining room candles, his place card made from a clamshell, the elegant pacing, the wines, Lila's odd speech about the Old Man, a late Calvados next to her by the fire. How it felt like they were all wrapped together inside this wonderful cocoon, so far from any civilization. It was Lila who had conceived and orchestrated the evening's structure, who had conjured its pre-Socratic depth, but when he complimented her she shrugged and changed the subject. It was not, perhaps, a night she would choose to remember. Wilkie did have, once or twice, the melancholy thought that these moments of perfection come more often toward the end of something rather than its beginning. Sitting together after a dinner like this, he and Lila would normally have laughed about the sad eclipse of finger-bowls, or some other signpost of the absurd prewar gentility, but tonight she was preoccupied. Stupidly, Wilkie had mentioned Baffin Island in an attempt to clear the air, and Lila had sunk even deeper into the fire. So, using his near-silent voice, Wilkie retreated to their one evergreen topic—the iniquities of Billy Quick, who was now at work on the fire five feet away from them.

But Lila was not listening. She saw a wall of trees in front of her, and Catta shivering. She wanted to run—to act somehow, *anyhow*—but it seemed that every possible way was blocked. She would scream, but she had guests.

There must be a path, Lila thought. There was always some way forward.

Billy knelt just in front of her, working on the fire, work which frankly struck her as unnecessary. He emptied all the logs from the box adjacent and lined them up by size, all the while holding a lit cigarette as if it were a flightless bird.

"Isn't it nice to have a fire?" she said to Wilkie, perhaps a touch too loud.

50

Catta had passed through the first and simplest stage of hunger, which is clarity, and was now into something new and more dangerous: call it phantasm. Only large, operatic gestures entered his mind.

He could walk into the ravine and ask the men for something to eat. Trespassers were often on some part of the property, which was much too big to police or patrol.

If these men were trespassers, they were unusually bold and well-informed ones—they had used a path on Baffin unknown to him or his family and had transported this machinery to a very remote part of the archipelago. They had sandwiches wrapped in wax paper, one of Martha's signatures. It was safer to assume that they belonged here, and that he too should act like he belonged. They might give him food. He also might have to run. He would stay low to the ground like a snake, and they would never catch him.

His one possible advantage was surprise. He would make a sudden entrance and appear at the top of the ravine. If he startled them, he would have more time to assess the situation. As he climbed down the boulder, though, his arm caught on a low branch and the branch snapped. Catta froze; his whole body listened for the whisper of a knife through air.

Disordered lights came up the path out of the ravine, and then three flashlights blinded Catta all at once. He hoped their silence meant confusion.

"Martha said I should get my dinner from you," Catta said before they had a chance to speak.

There was a long pause. One light flickered around in a circle, as if looking for other intruders. The others were in his eyes. The trees were very close.

"How'd you get here?" a harsh voice asked.

"I swam."

"Liar," the voice said.

"Everyone knows Martha," another voice said.

"We ain't got food just lying around."

"Peck didn't say no one was coming," another said.

"Peck also don't know nothing," the harsh-voiced one said.

"You one of Cyrus's boys?" another asked.

Name, rank, and serial number, Catta thought.

"My name is Catta Hillsinger."

"Family! Hell's bells."

"If we'd a known you was coming, we would of worn ties."

Two of them laughed and they briefly lowered their flashlights, which enabled him to see them in the light of the third. The taller one had the angry voice.

"Kinda name is Catta?" said one, and he recognized his voice as the man in charge in the ravine.

"Girl's name, I guess," the shorter one said.

"Sounds like a cat's name."

"Fancy."

"Kinda name a dog might give his stupid cat."

Two of the men laughed, but not the third. The third man, the tall one, looked furious. Catta hoped they were drunk.

"I came for the Migration," Catta said.

"See, Dale? See?" said the tall, harsh-voiced one. "They took the land from us, and now they want to take the Migration, too."

"Shut up, Conrad," the shorter man said.

"Family ain't welcome at the Migration," Dale, the leader, said to Catta.

That had been stupid—Catta knew North Island was off-limits to the families during the Migration. He was making mistakes. He had very few lies left before he had to tell the truth, and he couldn't waste them.

"I ran away," Catta said.

He was not sure where the lies were taking him or where they would end, but his only two choices were to keep talking or run.

"Who's your daddy?" the short one asked sharply.

Catta was silent. He had never come up against the limitations of his name before, but who could say what grudge they held against his father.

"Strange choice, running away to Baffin," the sarcastic one said.

"S'like running away to New Hampshire."

"Canada."

"Where's your boat?" the sarcastic one said.

"I swam," Catta said.

"Liar," Conrad said.

"What time?" Dale said.

"Just after three."

"Today?"

"Yesterday," Catta lied.

"Coulda done, tide being what it is. Barely."

"What you been eating?"

"Seaweed."

"Smock, give him your sandwich," Dale said.

"Now you gonna feed him?" Conrad said. "If you feed him, he stays here."

"He ain't on North, is he? Ain't nothing special about Baffin."

"Too close," Conrad said.

"Smock—sandwich."

"Never happen, Dale," Smock said.

"Do it."

Smock paused, and then he shuffled forward and handed over the wax paper package. Catta unwrapped it and ate half while standing there in front of them. It was just ham and cheese, but he recognized Martha's sourdough bread and it had the good mustard. These men were definitely not trespassers, but they were still dangerous. The sudden rush of warmth, after so much hunger, reminded him that he was cold, and that he should try to maintain a certain level of dignity. With great effort, he stopped himself from finishing the rest, rewrapped it and handed the sandwich back to Smock, who pocketed it.

"I'll pay you back," Catta said to him. "I got a fishing line out."

"Where at?" Dale said.

"Across from Seven."

"How long is it?"

"What?"

"The line."

"Three yards."

"Ain't no fish three yards in," Dale said. "Current's too strong, pulls 'em right across the center channel in either direction, except slack tide. You have that line out at noon?"

"No."

"No fish, then," Smock said.

"Turn around, boy," Dale said.

Catta turned, reluctantly.

Smock whistled.

"Damn, Dale," Smock said.

"Tried to bushwhack Baffin, hey?" Dale said.

"Serves him right," Conrad said.

Catta turned to face them and clasped his hands behind his back, as if to cover it retroactively.

"Is it bad?" he said.

51

It was after midnight and Edward Peck would have to be up again soon, but even so he used infinite care as he opened the Cottage door to avoid waking the children who he imagined were asleep upstairs. Instead, he found a circle of boys very much awake, sitting quietly in the darkened living room. A candle was lit in the middle of the circle, and the smallest boy lay asleep on his back with his mouth open. Peck asked James Hillsinger, the oldest boy present, to come outside with him.

"This is James Hillsinger," Peck said to George, the son of Billy Quick's unfortunate cousins, whom Peck had just picked up at the train station in Jennings. "James is a good man to ask about almost anything."

George, the new boy, had traveled without stopping for the last two days. He was handed off to new people at each stage of his journey, aunts and train conductors and now Edward Peck, and each person he had encountered had done roughly the same thing: handed him food, asked him nonsensical questions, and then taken him someplace new, where it all started over again with someone else.

Edward Peck carried George's suitcase up the stairs and into an attic room filled with bunk beds lined up in a row. George could not see the circle of boys as he passed upstairs, but he heard voices coming from the living room and wondered why anyone would still be up. In the bunk room, James—who had followed them up—pointed out an empty bed, whispering "That one" to keep from waking the younger boy who was asleep on a lower bunk with his arm hanging over and resting on the floor.

Edward Peck searched the closets and found one of the old scratchy wool blankets. Now, he thought gratefully, he could sleep for few hours before the Migration began at dawn.

"George, you are all squared away," Peck said to the new boy.

Finally, George thought. It was a small but important thing that Edward Peck said, since what George could not get from any of his handlers was a clear assessment of his immediate future. How long would he be on Seven? How long away from home? Some said three weeks, some longer or shorter; some wouldn't say at all. Also, he had never been on a boat before and was too embarrassed to say so. He knew that when Peck said he was *squared away* he was only talking about the bed, but even so Peck seemed to know a lot and he'd said it confidently, which made George feel like his future was more solid.

"Thank you," George said.

Peck walked down the stairs and out the screen door.

George knew it was late. He smiled at James, his latest benefactor, and waited for him to confirm that it was bedtime.

"Come with me," James said, and walked back down the stairs.

52

Catta walked behind the men on the narrow creek bed for what seemed like a long time. Dale, Conrad, and Smock each carried his own flashlight and a large jug of what Dale called *nectar*. They stopped often to change carrying hands. They asked him if he was still hungry, and Dale said they would feed him properly on North Island although he would have to leave promptly so as not to create a problem with a Hillsinger being on that island during the Migration. There was apparently an extremely serious rule about that, a rule that was handed down from Cyrus himself, and Conrad was furious. They were surprised when Catta said he would not leave Baffin. Smock asked him what his definition of *Baffin* was, and Catta was confused. Then Dale said, "How much water makes an island?" and Catta thought the question must be some kind of trick.

"Well," Dale said, "there's earth somewhere under everything. Even the deep trenches got a bottom six miles down."

Catta said, "OK, head-high water makes an island," and Conrad laughed. Conrad hated him.

"These islands is a miracle," Dale said. "That's certified. Your family—or I should say *both* families—they own the land. They got the paper. It's all arranged and tidy; there's no debate about that. Ain't no argument that the family can make certain rules. Paper says so, legislature says so. All agree. Even Conrad. But the Old Man ain't own the ways."

Dale paused.

"Before we go further," he continued, "do you promise you will keep the ways we show you to yourself—even if you *un*–run away or are otherwise once again taken into the corrupt bosom of the Hillsinger family—and I mean no offense?"

"Yes," Catta said.

"Raise your right hand and say it over again," Dale said, "so it's a valid contract in the State of Maine."

He repeated as much of what Dale had said as he could remember.

"Good enough," Dale said.

"Legislature can't fix sin," Conrad said.

"This is the Northern Path on Baffin Island," Dale said, ignoring Conrad. "It runs along the creek bed we been walking on, from North Island to near where, judging by what you said, your fishing line is right now catching jack-all. There might be another path, too, but we ain't gonna show you that one."

"He don't need to know the ways," Conrad said. "It's blasphemy."

53

George followed James downstairs into the Cottage living room. The boy who'd been asleep on the floor was awake now.

"Hello," George said to the assembled company.

There was no response, so George sat down at an open part of the circle.

"Stand up," James said.

George stood up.

"You are new to Seven Island."

"Yes!" George said. "I was never even on a boat before."

"Seven Island is a sacred place," James said. "Did you know that?"

"No, but I believe it," George said. These were the kinds of questions and answers he was used to from the last three weeks. He would smile often and agree to everything, and then eventually someone would bring him something to eat. Right now, he wanted to sleep.

"When you come to a sacred place for the first time," James said, "it's important to show your respect for its mysteries. I'm sure you know that."

"Yes, I do," George said.

"That's good," James said, and he nodded to one of the younger boys, who ran into the kitchen and returned with a tall glass full of something dark. The boy handed it to George.

"What is it?" George said.

"Something for you," James said.

All the boys murmured. It was hard for George to see it clearly in the light of the one candle. It was nearly full and fairly cool. It didn't smell like much.

"Did they all drink it?" George said about the other boys.

"They are all here," James said.

The screen door opened and slammed shut, and Penny Quick entered the living room, breathing hard. She thought it was odd that all the boys were still up.

"Who's he?" Penny said, pointing at George.

"Go on upstairs," James said.

Penny was furious. She had told herself that she would do anything necessary to keep up the fire on the headland, to keep the beacon lit for Catta, but she'd failed. She had been so tired and so hungry that she fell asleep next to the fire, and when she woke it was very cold because the fire had burnt down to ash. It was too dark to find more wood and Billy had kept the matches. She'd run the mile back on the road.

"What's that?" Penny said about the glass that George was still holding.

"It's not for you," James said.

"I asked you what it is," she said, desperate for a fight.

James didn't say anything.

"It's deer's blood!" one of the younger boys shouted, and they all exploded in long-suppressed laughter. George stepped away from his own hand but didn't drop the glass.

"I killed a deer this afternoon," James said, "especially for George."

Still panting from her run, Penny took the glass from George, and drank it. Then she walked outside into the tall grass and threw up.

The small boys all looked at James. He smiled.

"You're the Indian," James said to George.

54

March 1964
Camp Peary, Virginia

You ask me about a statue? Subotin said.

Yes—a bronze statue, Harris said. A statue of the Chekist Feliks Dzerzhinsky. When was it put up in front of KGB headquarters? What year?

Statues come, statues go, Subotin said. Who knows?

Hillsinger knew what a problem this question was for Subotin, although Subotin himself apparently did not. It was taken as axiomatic inside the CIA that all good KGB members would know exactly when the statue of Feliks Dzerzhinsky—Vladimir Lenin's first Chief of State Security—appeared outside their headquarters, since the CIA house view was that this particular decorating decision marked an explicit KGB turn, toward being more aggressive overseas. In theory, this belief was similar to the thought that all Americans would know where they were when they learned President Kennedy was shot. Whether any of it was true or not, here today the reality was that Harris was asserting, in a code understood very well by the CIA audience behind the glass, that Subotin was absolutely not who he said he was.

I ask again: how could you not know? Harris said.

No—I ask you, Subotin said. What is statue on top of U.S. Capitol building? Eh? Tell me.

According to Wise Men panel protocol, Harris was meant to be neutral, but in fact he was presenting the case for the prosecution— specifically, the case that Felix Subotin was a defector planted at the

CIA by the KGB to discredit the information of the earlier defector, Astrakhov. Harris was highlighting a list of inconsistencies in Subotin's earlier interviews, while behind the glass Cressie highlighted those moments that particularly contradicted Astrakhov's information. For Hillsinger, one or two of the disconnects were odd—he claimed to have information about foreign operations when he was nominally posted to the KGB's domestic-spying apparatus—but on the whole they were minor, well within the scope of normal defector anomalies. As a rule, defectors exaggerated their own access and value. The Counterintelligence view, however, seemed to be that the sheer weight of these inconsistencies would do two things: one, prove that Subotin was a false defector maliciously sent to spread disinformation; and/or, two, scare any of the assembled Wise Men away from taking Subotin's side of the argument in any internal debate. The strategy seemed to be working especially well on Danziger, the man from the Far East division.

Subotin is a massive fraud, Danziger said, behind the one-way glass. It's terrifying he got this far into the system.

And now we come to Oswald and the assassination of President Kennedy, Harris said, on the other side of the glass.

While under normal circumstances this might have been explosive material, Hillsinger and other senior staff were all aware the agency had already come to the view that the KGB could not be definitively linked to the assassination. The one thing everyone in that room already knew about Subotin was that he had confirmed the preexisting consensus of KGB noninvolvement.

Yes, Oswald, Subotin said. I already tell this a thousand times. KGB think Oswald crazy, they interview him but don't pursue anything. Anyway, when in Soviet Union Oswald is living in Minsk. Minsk is shithole, no dangerous spy live in Minsk. Nobody want to expel him, though, because to expel someone takes a lot of departments, very dangerous politically, and nobody think this crazy American is worth risking his career. So Oswald file is passed to million people, nobody want it, everyone keep passing it on. I do this myself for same reason.

Harris and Subotin rehashed the Oswald material that everyone already knew.

They ask me for a recommendation on Oswald, Subotin said. I say don't expel, too many headaches. Send him home. Give him name of someone to contact in U.S. so he feel like big man. I suggest Hans Kallenbach, but my supervisor say no, that contact is sensitive. I think they make up a name and phone number in New York and send Oswald to airport.

Hillsinger had leaned forward at the mention of Hans Kallenbach. This, surely, was deep Counterintelligence material that Angleton had not meant to expose.

Yes, yes, Kallenbach, Harris said. We already know about him.

Who the hell is Hans Kallenbach? Todd, the Office of Security man, said to Cressie back behind the glass.

A third party who Moscow uses to move money in the States, Cressie said. He's a Swiss national, so we're constrained.

At the time, Hillsinger knew Kallenbach's name only slightly, as a contact of Peregrine Wilkie's. Several years earlier, Hillsinger had been told by a friendly FBI contact—off-the-record and as a courtesy—that Hannah Quick was about to be summoned to the New York City Board of Education to answer questions about her membership in the Communist Party. Hillsinger had immediately called Peregrine Wilkie from a pay phone, and Peregrine in turn had sent John Wilkie to Hannah and Billy's apartment in Harlem to negotiate a surrender. When Hillsinger saw John Wilkie for lunch later that month, Wilkie had outlined the terms, which Hillsinger thought were unduly favorable. Wilkie had also listed the investors Peregrine had recruited, including Hans Kallenbach, who at the time had just moved to New York to open the American branch of Kallenbach Bros., an exclusive private bank out of Zurich. Wilkie said all the best Europeans had vouched for Kallenbach. Hillsinger's own impression was that he was a playboy first and financier second.

Show them my cell, Subotin said to Harris, pointing at the glass.

You don't have a cell, Harris said. You have a room.

Ask him to see it, Subotin said to the men behind the glass. Ask Harris why important KGB defector is kept in jail. Ask him why this man is tortured.

Are you ready to continue? Harris said. It's time to talk about Mexico City.

55

When James said, "You're the Indian," George had not moved until one of the small boys jumped up and screamed, "Run!"

He walked calmly to the door. Outside, Penny knelt at the side of the house, drinking water from the hose.

"What does it mean when they say I'm the Indian?" George said.

"It means run."

Penny took off up the hill, and George ran after her in his dress shoes. They stopped at the base of a tree just opposite the barn, only about three hundred yards away from the Cottage porch. Penny climbed it in the dark and called down to him where the next hand- or foothold was: six inches left or just beside the small branch with one leaf. Soon they arrived at a high perch where two small people could sit with their backs against the tree trunk and see the barn and the Cottage, as well as the harbor and most of the clearing on this side of the hill. It occurred to him that Penny had done this before.

She said that if and when the boys found him, they would beat him until they got bored, but only below the neck. The Indian Game had no known end point other than that. Usually the runner gave up and suffered the consequences—which were better or worse depending on James's mood—rather than living out the night in the barren woods around the clearing. The boundaries and other rules changed each time, she said, again according to James's whim, since the oldest boy had the privilege of making the rules: only he decided how long the runner's head start was or whether he was allowed to wear shoes or a shirt or any clothes at all. If adults appeared, birdcalls went out that were amazingly lifelike—somehow all the boys could do it. By rule, girls were excluded, Penny said, but some nights she had come out and watched the game from this tree. James always checked the hayloft first, since the younger boys always panicked and hid in the first good place they saw. Penny said they would not make that same mistake.

56

Catta left the woods and walked onto the beach. The ocean was immense. The riot of space, the stars and birds, the massive wind and water. He was sure he could see every star ever created.

The gully path had ended and they bushwhacked the last stretch of forest before emerging onto the beach directly opposite North Island, whose hills rose up across the wide channel. Conrad pulled a canoe from the woods and dragged it over the rocks to the water. Catta's father had said they would return for him at three seventeen P.M. Catta had said *What should I eat?* and his father had pointed in the two directions, woods and water. Still, he could not bring himself to get into the canoe. He would not be rescued.

Dale turned toward him in the lighter darkness of the shore.

"You don't object to following us on Baffin?"

"No."

"You don't object to walking?"

"No."

"And you're hungry?" Dale said.

"Yes."

"Watch," Dale said.

There was an oblong rock at the tree line and Dale knelt down and drew an invisible line out along the point of it, toward the eastern hill on North Island. He walked into the water, along that invisible line.

Catta expected him to pitch over any second, to be sucked under and away, but Dale kept walking—ten yards, fifty, a hundred, shining his flashlight down every few feet to show that the water never passed his knees. Soon Catta could see only the bobbing light, which then began to rise: Dale had reached North Island and climbed up to level ground.

"It's a path sixty minutes before and sixty after low tide," Smock said.

Conrad launched the canoe loaded with the three jugs, while Catta followed Smock onto the tidal road. The water was shockingly cold, much colder now than during the day. The men all had waterproof waders on, but his sneakers were soaked and heavy and he could move only slowly since, being shorter, the water rose nearly to his waist. Out in the middle of the channel, standing almost on top of the ocean, he was closer to the stars than he had ever dreamt he would be. He cupped his hands and splashed the cold seawater onto his entire body, cleaning off the dirt and blood of the other journey, the one that had taken him from the open sea to the heart of Baffin. Up ahead, Smock shouted for him to keep up, and Catta shuffled on as fast as he could.

57

Lila had never seen Billy Quick sit so quietly, or do any one thing for so long, as he worked on the fire just in front of her. He was wholly focused on arranging logs, adding sticks, small adjustments, building what appeared to be a burning tripod, a shape not unlike the wigwams from old picture books. That was a word she loved: *wigwam*. Years ago, a friend of her father's had built what he called a *yurt* by the water all the way out on Long Island, farther even than Montauk, near the preposterous cliffs. The friend was a lapsed archaeologist, an eccentric, and there was some minor point of Asian ethnography to the yurt, although in her mind it was a wigwam. Hannah had made such a fuss about sleeping in it that her parents and the archaeologist had finally agreed to let her do it. Lila had not wanted to seem more scared than her younger sister, so she joined her. The yurt smelled like old leather (which it was), and, perversely, it reminded Lila of the enormous green chairs in the library of the Knickerbocker Club, which she was allowed to sit in once a year on her birthday, drinking hot chocolate with marshmallows. That whole night Lila was absolutely terrified—alive to every sound, afraid of the crickets even, dreading some apocalypse. Her one consolation was the bellbuoy out in Long Island Sound, a friendly noise among the imagined strangers and creaking trees. Hannah, of course, slept through the night without moving. *Good morning, sunshine*, she'd said, long after the sun was up. Lila doubted that her sister would have told Billy about that particular trip. It was nothing; it was barely even conversation. From Hannah's fearless perspective, it was a lark and not a trial.

Wilkie asked a question that Lila did not hear, but she nodded reflexively and he left. She was glad to have a certain amount of space around her for a moment, and she imagined Baffin again, the same wall of trees and the same shivering. She would stay as close as possible to this pain; she owed it to Catta that if she could not change the situation, she would at the very least meditate on it unceasingly. Diana would argue that thoughts were a form of action. In front of her, Billy loudly emptied the box of firewood and threw the last bark and sticks into the fire. He turned back toward her and pointed to a little figure on the hearth he must have built while she was looking away. It was just three sticks leaning together.

"You slept in a wigwam once," Billy said. He said it softly, intimately, in a voice almost indistinguishable from the background noise. She could easily have pretended not to hear.

"I did," Lila said. "I loved it."

There it is, Billy thought. *In heaven, everyone will talk like that.*

In the time of their meetings, he'd often thought she was barely tolerating him. She had ended whatever it was without ceremony, even without notification. This was a very different Lila—her voice just now was darker, lower, more powerful than it normally was. Wholly uncontrived. *Inviting.* He hesitated to say it, but that was what he'd heard. And yet—given the potential gravity of this change, it would be irresponsible not to ask—could he have heard her wrong? Was she merely tired or distracted? Was there distortion in the room, a hidden echo? *No*, he thought. Emphatically not. There was a depth of resignation in her voice, an almost unwilling knowledge, clear evidence of a struggle prior to the Baffin situation. Some veil had lifted, if only for a moment. Billy Quick hated mysticism in all its many forms, but it was nevertheless true that with Lila, only the vanishing images were real. He had heard the Old Man say many times *In this room we speak the truth*, so however improbable his conclusion might be, he would let it stand for now. What Billy Quick had seen, what he thought he heard inside those three nothing words *I loved it*, was the raised flag of Lila's surrender. To him.

58

March 1964
Camp Peary, Virginia

It was now Sunday afternoon. Subotin's debrief was over. The practice of Wise Men panels was to reach a conclusion immediately after all primary material had been disclosed. Cressie would ask for opinions, and then they would vote.

Mr. Danziger, Cressie said.

Subotin is a fraud, Danziger said. Moscow sent him to discredit Astrakhov. His awareness of us is too good and his resistance to interrogation too complete for him to be untrained. He's clearly a professional, and we know that the KGB doesn't send staff officers as false defectors, so his resume is certainly faked. That explains some of the inconsistencies, and the fact that we've heard nothing about this operation through other channels would suggest that it was restricted to the top level in Moscow. That would also explain the huge resources they've put in the field here—a lot of work has gone into this guy, a lot of background. We're lucky he slipped up a few times. Frankly, we're fortunate that Counterintelligence was on top of this.

At the CIA, Hillsinger thought, they wanted to believe the Russians were free from all internal inefficiencies, doubts, restrictions, as if they were the reverse image of us. As if totalitarianism had produced in Moscow the Platonic intelligence service. It was a lie.

Mr. Todd, Cressie said.

The inconsistencies concern me, Todd said, as do the gaps in internal KGB knowledge. He knows both too much and too little. He does not know the things he ought to—like when the Dzerzhinsky statue went up—and his overseas knowledge bears no relationship to his stated positions. It seems most likely that he's some guy, a freelancer, who they trained up partway. He knows enough to be credible but not to sustain hostile interrogation like this. He's a botched project, and we caught him thanks to the strong questioning.

Between them, Hillsinger thought, Danziger and Todd had just articulated the Counterintelligence view of Subotin. They had both reached the conclusion that Angleton had designed this exercise to produce—that Subotin was a double agent, a provocation, a closely held KGB operation. Subotin was chaos and confusion, set against the clarity of Astrakhov. This Wise Men panel, Hillsinger reckoned, was intended as a minor formality en route to Astrakhov's briefing of the President.

For Hillsinger, though, the case was not convincing. The current debrief had been heavily slanted toward the gaps and inconsistencies in Subotin's story, but then the truth most often had a rough surface. The defectors who scared him were the ones with perfect stories.

Mr. Hillsinger, Cressie said.

So which is it? Hillsinger said. By Danziger's lights, the KGB is an organization of supermen who make no mistakes, who conceived this elaborate provocation and almost pulled it off, or—as Todd says—they are a bunch of amateurs who sent a botched project to do the most dangerous job they have. We can't have it both ways.

And your own view, Mr. Hillsinger? Cressie said.

Hillsinger knew that a minority view was not what Angleton or, for that matter, the Director would want from this panel at all. Anything less than unanimity would cause the Director to table the recommendation for the near term. Angleton would be furious.

What does Astrakhov think? Hillsinger asked Cressie. Hillsinger knew the answer, but he wanted to see what Angleton had authorized his team to disclose.

Astrakhov, Cressie said, actually predicted the appearance of Subotin, or of someone like him. He said that Moscow would certainly send out one or more false defectors to discredit him.

Has Astrakhov seen the Subotin material? Hillsinger said.

Some of it, Cressie said.

That, Hillsinger thought, was a massive tactical error. Cressie had just admitted a violation of applicable CIA policies and possibly several laws—they had disclosed classified information to an unauthorized person. In a courtroom, this case would be thrown out right there.

So to summarize, Hillsinger said, we have shown a known KGB agent the take from a secret KGB source attempting to defect?

Only when it conflicted with Astrakhov's own information, Cressie said.

I see, Hillsinger said. Meanwhile, we have effectively created a situation where Astrakhov is one hundred percent incentivized to reject Subotin's information as false.

That's irrelevant, Danziger said. We're making this decision today, not Astrakhov.

Hillsinger wondered if his exposure of the preposterous bias of this panel—which was now established beyond doubt—would make any difference to the official voting, which was still to come. Would the Director really have sanctioned a show trial like this? Did he know what was happening here?

Actually, Hillsinger said, it seems to me that Counterintelligence has already made this decision. Everything we have seen the last three days suggests that the present interrogation is hostile. This special cabin, the handcuffs. One does not undertake hostile interrogations unless one already believes the subject to be lying. Therefore, Counterintelligence has prejudged the case.

What we have done—Cressie began, but Hillsinger interrupted him.

Here is my assessment, he said, since you've asked: in my view, both

Astrakhov and Subotin are legitimate, in the sense that they are both former employees of the KGB who are legitimately attempting to escape the Soviet Union. It strikes me as unlikely that either is being controlled by Moscow. But—and this is crucial—they are also both much smaller fish than we have been led to believe. The information of both should be treated with suspicion. And as far as this panel is concerned, let me state for the record that Subotin is not a case of deception; he is a case of nepotism and bureaucratic incompetence.

How so? Todd said.

Subotin, Hillsinger said, is a celebrity's son that the KGB let into the service, most likely without proper vetting. He did not live up to expectations. Worse, he was a liability—both professionally and, more important, politically. As such, he was shunted around to different departments and denied any real information, while all of his supervisors tried simultaneously to avoid both firing him and giving him any real responsibility. And now, here with us, he's tried to inflate his own importance and hide his lack of success. Subotin's entire case is consistent with that interpretation.

You're about this close, Danziger said, to being an enemy of the state.

As for Astrakhov, Hillsinger continued, right now his entire life is dependent on our patronage; if you were him—if you had access to the highest levels at the CIA and your entire life and future depended on keeping that privileged access—wouldn't you do everything to avoid being supplanted as the official CIA oracle? Wouldn't you predict that Moscow would send false defectors to discredit you, and wouldn't you try to cannibalize anyone who came over afterward?

Are you accusing Astrakhov of being dirty? Danziger said.

No, Hillsinger said. I'm accusing him of being human.

There was a heavy silence.

The question for your consideration, Cressie said—he was using the official formula now, which meant they were voting for the record—is this: is Subotin a legitimate defector? Yes means we accept Subotin's information. No means we do not accept it. Yes means bona fide, No means not bona fide. Inconclusive is self-explanatory.

Can we have a bit more time? Todd said.

Delay is not in my instruction set, Cressie said. I'll bring in a third-party witness to certify the polling of this panel.

Cressie went out and returned with Harris, Subotin's interrogator, who did not say anything.

Now I'll begin the polling, Cressie said. Mr. Danziger?

No, Danziger said.

Mr. Danziger—no, Cressie said. Subotin not bona fide. Mr. Hillsinger?

Yes, Hillsinger said.

Mr. Hillsinger—yes, Cressie said. Subotin bona fide. Mr. Todd?

There was a pause.

Inconclusive, Todd said.

59

When Catta reached dry land, Conrad handed him one of the big glass nectar jugs to carry. It was heavy and it smelled like sweat, raspberries, and gasoline.

"Go slow," Conrad said.

It was darker on North than on the Baffin shore, and there was no light anywhere on the horizon apart from the slender moon, nothing to be seen except for the stars.

"Where?" Catta said.

"Walk straight for the tail of the Big Bear," Conrad said, "and for Christ's sake go slow."

Catta's shoes and shorts were soaked and he was already shivering as he set out toward Orion with the jug slung over his shoulder. He walked over a small rise and then he saw a fire in a sunken pit, which was itself inside a larger depression. The fire was so low down that from the other side he had not seen even its glow.

"Gently now," Smock said to Catta as he put the jug down. Dale opened a can and poured its contents into a large cast-iron pan and placed the pan directly on top of the fire. It smelled more than good.

"Won't they see the fire from Seven?" Catta said as he climbed almost into the fire to get warm.

"Fire stays below the rises," Dale said. "Family ain't to know we're on the property."

All three of them, Dale said, had a long time ago been regular staff on Seven Island, before Catta was born. They had all had been fired—or, as Dale said, *terminated for various voluptuous offenses*. At present, they were "officially" (though also secretly, Smock said, as far as Billy Quick and the rest of the family were concerned) hired to tattoo numbers onto the ears of the new lambs and write those numbers in a small notebook. Unofficially, Dale said, they brewed the nectar and organized all the other *peremptories* that sustained the many different facets of the festival of the Migration.

"Full-service and humane flock accountability, state-of-the-art tattooing all numbers but one," Smock said.

Conrad came over the rise and let his jug fall heavily next to the other one.

"Careful now," Smock said to him.

"Stop lying to the boy and lift something," Conrad said.

"Hospitality is my cross to bear," Dale said cheerfully.

Conrad left, heading back toward the beach.

"Why not the number one?" Catta said.

"Conrad don't know how to write it," Smock said.

"Excuse me," Dale said. "I meant to say there is *one number* we don't tattoo, but it ain't the number *one*."

"Seven," Smock said.

Catta could not see the logic of that, and said so.

"Leave it that seven by itself is bad luck," Dale said. "Not seventeen and not forty-seven—just seven alone. Small point of doctrine. You will not see a lamb on these islands with a seven in its ear."

They both laughed when Catta asked what else their church believed. Dale picked up a filthy oven mitt, pulled the pan from the fire, and placed it, smoking and popping, on the ground in front of him.

"Smock?"

"I ain't—"

"Get the man a fork," Dale said.

"Pardon, pardon," Smock said, and he disappeared over the rise behind them, toward a shack whose roof, Catta could see now, was the mass hiding the stars just above the horizon.

"It's basic," Dale said. "Lambs is important; lambs is exceptional. All fires shall have fragrant smoke. Wakefulness. Songs. Contortions of the host. At the Migration we sing together, to be heard in other places."

Smock returned, out of breath, and wiped the fork on his jacket before handing it to Catta. The pan held franks and beans that were scaldingly hot. Catta blew three or four times on each forkful and then ate so fast and so greedily that Dale and Smock laughed at him, which made him stop. He offered the pan back to them.

"No, sir—no, thank you. Good riddance to them beans," Dale said.

They said Catta was welcome to any food they had and welcome to share their fire and their water (though not the nectar, which was only for the congregation). Dale said, however, that it would be both a sacrilege and an insult if Catta or any other member of either family were to be either on or near North Island between sunrise on the day of the Migration and the sunrise after that. Which, Dale said, gave him a limited number of minutes before the tide rose to walk the tidal path back to Baffin, or somewhat more minutes if they ferried him back by canoe. The choice was his.

Conrad returned to the circle with another jug, which he let fall heavily again.

"He can swim hisself back," Conrad said.

60

In the tree above the barn, Penny asked George for his shoe. He took it off and handed it to her. Below them, down on the ground, James had led the little ones up from the Cottage to the barn in a swarm of flashlights. After a few minutes, a girl's voice had shouted inside and some of the boys had run out laughing. Then they saw Sheila shove a small boy out the barn's side door, followed by James, who was too big for her to shove.

"Just answer the question," James said.

"No," Sheila said. "No one else came in here."

"We need five minutes to check the stalls and the loft," James said.

"Don't go near Betsy's box—the puppies don't like the flashlight."

James went back inside with two other boys.

"Can we see the new lamb?" one of the littler boys asked her outside the barn.

"There's three new lambs," Sheila said.

"Is there one who's also a dog?"

"He's sleeping."

The boy said they would happily look in the dark.

Once they all went back inside, Penny tossed George's shoe out of their tree. It landed halfway between the tree line and the hayloft rope.

James reemerged from the loft, shouted, "It's clear!" and all the little ones came streaming out the side door.

One of them found George's shoe right away; there was

more shrieking and another one said, "He's barefoot and wounded."

James said, "Check the woods," and the boys headed directly under them on a path into the forest.

Once their flashlights had all disappeared, Penny said "OK" to George and began to climb down again, telling him which handholds and footholds to use. She crossed the few yards of empty space to the barn and climbed the knotted rope up into the hayloft. George started downhill to retrieve his shoe, but Penny said, "Leave it," and he did.

"Throw your other shoe way down the hill toward the water," she said.

George took off the other shoe and threw it toward the Cottage, but then the flashlights appeared again in the woods, moving fast.

"Look out!" Penny hissed from the loft, not wanting to shout.

She heard the voice of James shout, "There he is," and the flashlights were all on him and then George was covered in angry boys.

"Only below the neck," she heard James say.

61

What Lila needed now was consecrated ground. She stood up from the sofa intending to flee, but then suddenly they all wanted her: Diana, Wilkie, even Christopher Templeton. Everyone converged, said the dinner had been wonderful, astonishing, et cetera. She smiled and thanked them all effusively and walked out, running only when she heard the heavy front door close behind her. The outdoor chapel was in a little grove cut out of the forest down by the water. Its benches were split logs and the altar a stump still embedded in the ground; from time to time, family members were married or eulogized there. Lila stopped at the edge of the grove to catch her breath but also to make sure she was alone, since the chapel was also known to be a place for trysts.

She sat down on the bench farthest from the water. She had seen Jim watch her leave from his post across the room, but he would not come after her. He put too high a price on his own solitude to steal it from someone else. The real question was whether he had seen or heard, from across the room, the obscene thing that escaped from her there in front of the fire? Was some version of it visible on her face?

The words themselves were inconsequential. She had said *I loved it* about the silly wigwam out past Montauk when in fact she had been terrified of it, something Billy apparently already knew. If there was a thread of conspiracy in those words—or some sort of invitation in her tone—then could it not be argued, setting aside their recent history, that she had known Billy half her life? That he had loved her sister, and so had she? Was it not true, she asked the high tribunal of whichever gods presided here, that this same innocent dynamic—a loss they shared—was what had sent them down that other path in the first place? And that—whatever had happened between their bodies—she had nevertheless always kept him at the appropriate distance? Why would she now feel something she did not feel then, when it would have been so much easier to have been legitimately in love with Billy Quick? It made no sense.

And yet her voice had betrayed her. She had not used or felt anything like that tone, since that first night with Jim in Merion by the fountain. It was involuntary, a prosecuter might argue, which made it definitive. And in fact, she had taken the very existence of that sound, that tone, to be the first objective sign that she was in love. Had it lied to her this time? She had to ask, Lila told herself, because in this particular case, it was impossible for her to be in love with Billy Quick. It must be something else.

62

"The number seven," Catta said.

There was confusion in their faces.

"You can't be here after dawn," Dale said. "And dawn comes quick this close to the solstice."

"You start across the shallow path now," Smock said.

Catta said he was eager to begin walking, just as soon as they helped him with this inconsequential thing: he wanted a tattoo of the number seven on his upper left arm. The men exploded.

"—stupid stupid stupid—"

"—anyone named Hillsinger—"

"—irreligious—"

"—unwholesome—"

"—bad luck—"

Catta laughed. He knew they didn't want to do it, but he found himself not caring. He said he wished there was more time to explain, but the tide was filling in the path.

"It's sacrilege," Conrad said.

"Show me how and I'll do it myself," Catta said.

Again the three men spoke all at once:

"—ain't so easy—"

"—risk of infection—"

"—unprofessional—"

"I'll say *I* did it," Catta said, "with squid ink and a fishing hook."

Smock stood up and spat.

"Never seen a squid here this time of year," he said.

Now Dale, too, looked at Catta in a harsh way that surprised him.

"Cyrus won't like it if the boy's on North after sunrise, much less when the barge comes," Dale said, turning toward Catta. "That's the rest of it, ain't it?"

"If my name wasn't Hillsinger, you would do it," Catta said.

"If your name weren't Hillsinger, we'd throw you into the sea," Conrad said.

"Now we're talking professional services," Dale said, "and in that case we'll need payment."

"I don't have any money," Catta said.

"Need another canoe paddle."

Catta wasn't sure how he would get one, but at this stage he would have agreed to anything.

"Done."

"Need a mess of birch bark."

"Fine," Catta said.

"Know how much a mess is, Hillsinger?"

"Yes."

"Also need ten more cans of—"

"Nah," Conrad said. "That's stealing from Martha."

"Fair enough," Dale said. "Canoe paddle, birch bark, and silence to the grave. All points nonnegotiable."

The tattoo itself was fast and spectacularly painful. It turned out that Conrad was the acknowledged expert, and none of them spoke while he made seven small dots on Catta's upper left arm with what looked like a small sewing needle that he put in the fire after dipping it in ink and before each impression. Dale poured alcohol over the marks. Smock laughed when he cried out. When it was done, Conrad handed him a blanket with holes in it. Catta stood up to leave, and none of them said anything. He walked over the rise in silence, with the thread-bare wool blanket over his neck.

On the shallow path back to Baffin, the water ran all the way up to his chest now. He could feel the tide building, slowly pushing him off the high road and into the deep trenches. His arm stung where the tattoo was, but Cyrus said salt water healed everything. Looking back at North, there was no sign of the men or their fire. Even the glow was invisible.

63

George built a sort of nest in the hayloft, and he hoped from the outside it would look like hay bales thrown haphazardly into the loft. There was an old blanket hanging on a nail, which he put at the center and then made a small opening on the other side, for ventilation. Penny was sure that even if James and the smaller boys came back they would never find them, even if they had flashlights.

Once the boys had finished with George, they moved in a body back down the hill to the Cottage. There was no way he would sleep in that house tonight, among those cowards. George had lashed out and hit a few of them, although it was dark and he couldn't see which ones he got or where he got them. He hoped they had bruises, so he could tell later who they were. He hoped one of them was James.

"Did it hurt much?" Penny had said.

"No," George had said.

Penny climbed into the tiny space that smelled like dust and grass and horses, like the rough edges of a summer. George crawled in after her and lay down on the scratchy wool blanket and found an angle they both could tolerate.

64

Catta woke with the sun. He lay on a small patch of moss just off Baffin's rocky beach, next to the channel separating him from Seven. He had recrossed Baffin along the dry creek bed in the dark, and it was hard: the path ended at the base of the ravine, where the machine was, and after that the creek-bed was overgrown and sometimes ambiguous. Several times he had to kneel down to feel with his hands for the small differences in grade between the surrounding forest and the path. Then it had stopped altogether. Soon he'd heard water on stones and then fought through the last dense, overlapping waves of pines to the rocky shore opposite Seven Island. Penny's fire was out. It was not even smoking anymore. He heard an engine in the distance—it must be a lobsterman, he thought, which made him think of the Migration. All the sheep would run down the hill sometime after sunrise. He wondered if he would hear the gun.

Now he owed a debt: a canoe paddle and birch bark, to be delivered at the end of the Starks Cove dock on Seven proper. Meanwhile, his father had said he would reappear at three seventeen P.M. on the Baffin beach where they had left him. Yesterday seemed like years ago. He had two options: to leave, pay his debt, and keep moving, or stay on Baffin and let his father shake his hand and say *How was it?* or *You're late* or even *Well done.* Even the idea of it was ridiculous.

Catta shouted to a cormorant flying through the channel, and the cormorant turned its head and answered back. His luck would never get better than that.

65

May 1964
Georgetown, Washington, D.C.

The end began with a lunch invitation. Hillsinger was summoned to the house of Michael Forrest for lunch on a Saturday, which was not sinister in itself. Forrest had been Chief of Station in Warsaw when Hillsinger was posted there. They were still closely in touch, and the summons had come with enough lead time to be plausibly social. Forrest's wife had opened the door and offered him Scotch on a silver tray. She was Japanese and distantly related to Emperor Hirohito, which had apparently caused clearance problems when Forrest married her.

Forrest sat on the back porch at a table elegantly set for two. A tube in his nose was attached to an oxygen tank on wheels, and he was smoking an unfiltered cigarette. After a long career that had included several important posts overseas, Forrest had been, for a short time, the Deputy Director of Plans, the top operational job at the CIA. He resigned less than a year into it due to advanced emphysema. It was unusual for anyone to leave that particular job both alive and without controversy, but his medical condition was a special circumstance. Forrest continued to be well-informed, since the Director found it convenient to use him as a back channel to less savory elements in the global intelligence community. As Forrest himself put it, that was a smart strategy on the Director's part. The messenger would be dead inside of a year.

Perfect day, Forrest said.

Paradise, Hillsinger said.

Did you bring that champagne I mentioned? Forrest said.

Hillsinger paused to make sure he had heard correctly.

Akiko put it in the freezer, Hillsinger said. I'm afraid it got warm on the way over.

I'll remind her, Forrest said.

In Poland, he and Forrest had agreed that any extracontextual use of the term champagne *would be code for present danger: surveillance, deception, imminent enemy action.*

Forrest spoke to his wife in Japanese. A moment later, the sound of very loud opera floated out of the living room windows.

Is it that bad? Hillsinger said.

It's worse, Forrest said. He lit another cigarette.

Are they here in the bushes? Hillsinger said.

Forgive me for being short, Forrest said. We have limited time, so let's make sure their basic facts are correct.

Who is they*? Hillsinger said.*

The people neither of us want them to be.

Are we on the record here?

Of course not.

Are you officially sanctioned?

Do I look official to you?

Are you wired?

No. That's why we're using Puccini to defeat your surveillance.

My surveillance*? Hillsinger said.*

Wake up, Forrest said. I will ask, and you will answer. Were you or were you not recruited this year for an intradepartmental Wise Men panel on the Subotin defection?

Hillsinger did not speak. He was not worried yet, although he had to assume, despite assurances, that Forrest was recording this conversation and that anything he said would be admissible either in court or as part of an internal tribunal. He had been part of those. He had seen it done.

I take it from your silence, Forrest said, that you're concerned about my clearance. You're wondering if I might be on their side, or possibly an unwitting pawn. That's fair. Let us operate on the premise that you will do nothing when things I say are true, and you will drink from your water glass when things are false.

It would obviously be a very serious thing, Hillsinger said, to divulge classified or operational information to any individual not holding official clearance.

I appreciate your candor, Forrest said, so I will match it. If you take that approach, you'll end up in jail.

Yes, Hillsinger said. I was recruited for the Subotin Wise Men panel.

By the Director? Forrest said.

Yes.

Himself?

Yes.

What did he say, exactly? Forrest said.

He said he wanted me to go to the Farm to look at a defector. He said to block out the weekend.

What did you find when you got there? Forrest said.

First, a pile of memos summarizing the views of the first defector, Astrakhov.

Was there anything odd about them?

It seemed like Angleton was giving a lot away.

Did that concern you?

Personally? No.

Why not? Forrest said.

I assumed the Director had ordered it.

Have you ever heard of anyone in Counterintelligence, let alone Angleton himself, asking for a Wise Men panel?

Hillsinger did not answer the question.

The memos you read were fakes, Forrest said. The details, the troop counts, the contingency plans. All fabrications. Did that possibility occur to you?

No.

Did you really have no sense of danger?

Hillsinger drank from his water glass.

There is a memo, Forrest continued, in restricted circulation. Only the Director and three or four others have seen it. This memo is from Angleton's shop. It contains the names of five senior CIA staff who are, in the view of Counterintelligence, prime candidates for what they believe to be one or more high-level KGB penetrations of the CIA.

And? Hillsinger said.

Your name is on top of the list.

66

Penny opened her eyes. There were low voices in the barn. George was awake, looking out through a gap in the hay bales.

Penny sat up and climbed out, waving for George to stay. She crept along the one firm, uncreaking plank to the end of the loft, where she could see down into the stalls. She was surprised to see Cyrus's son Matthew. Then she heard Sheila, who was the opposite of calm.

"He can come back here—Edward Peck can bring him back," Matthew said, "but the tattooing is only on North."

"He ain't going."

"His momma's on the barge. Betsy works today."

"He's been sleeping with the puppies—he smells like dog. The other sheep'll push him off."

"Cyrus says you got to come to North, too."

"I can't."

There was a pause.

Then Sheila was shrieking *no no no*. Matthew must have approached the little dog bed where Colt was, maybe tried to take the newborn with him by force. Then the barn door opened and closed and Penny could hear Sheila breathing hard. Everything else was quiet.

67

"You must have been cold," Jim said when Lila came in shortly after dawn.

She took off her dress and lay down next to him.

"Yes," she said. "I was cold."

Lila could not, in fact, remember if she had been cold or not. It would have been better to be cold. As it was, she was merely clear: she was in love with Billy Quick. She had fought all night against it—against the feeling that had driven her out of the living room, out of her bed, even out of the Seven Chapel. She'd prayed as a last resort, but even her prayers were lies. She was in love with Billy Quick.

Lila had felt, there in front of the fire, when she had said *I loved it*, something like an intuition of survival—this preposterous joy. She could feel its velocity even now. It was no longer possible for her to say that Billy Quick was not involved, for example that he was an effect rather than the cause.

What followed this velocity, though, what it inevitably produced, was paralysis. Her guilt absorbed everything—all bravery, all thirst for action. Her husband stood accused of treason. The name *Lila Hillsinger* was on secret lists in secret offices in at least two countries, and as far away as Moscow. Organizations with vast resources had acted against her. Her son was shivering on an island that other children thought as terrifying as a graveyard. Her sister was dead. Lila had left a trail of, if not destruction, certainly of agony.

And yet, to her eternal shame what most troubled her now was that she did not know exactly what Billy Quick had thought, during her moment of weakness there in front of the fire. He was an observant man, fully capable of parsing shadows. He would have noticed.

68

Catta stood at the water's edge for a long time. The sky was pink and the moving water was cold. He took off his heavy shoes and what remained of his shirt and waded out twenty feet. Then he dove.

The current caught him when he was still underwater, and when Catta came up, his breathing was out of control. He was instantly both tired and afraid. Penny's headland went by too quickly, and then he passed the long, sharp edge of Sisters, going too fast, still swimming but being carried sideways into the bay at high speed. His fingers and toes were numb now, and there was a distance in his limbs, as if they belonged to someone else. This kind—this *depth* of cold was new. How long could he last? Ahead of him was the bay, wide and crescent-shaped, with the Long Beach on one side and the Atlantic on the other. As it was now, there was nothing to stop the current from taking him straight past the beach and out of the bay into the open sea. There was no land to speak of between Seven Island and Spain, and if he were to let go for just a moment, if he would simply drift, then the tide would carry him across the ocean. The Spaniards would find his broken corpse. They would see the number seven on his arm. They would be amazed.

And then his luck changed. Catta fought the current into the mouth of the bay, the wide water enclosing the Long Beach, and at the mouth it broadened out somewhat, its force diffused, the concentration less. He made some progress toward the beach. That was better, but he could not relax—this change might not be real, his reprieve could be just an eddy. The tide could easily be waiting for him closer to the shore. He pulled harder, to build momentum. He was closer to the beach now than he had been sixty seconds ago, which was good, but Catta still had a clear sense of the water all around him moving backward, of the tide's enormous wishes guiding him out to sea. Then all around him, everything went slack. He pulled deeper, kicked harder, put all reserves into a last push toward the beach. When his feet finally touched bottom, Catta paused for a few seconds there in the freezing surf, trying to breathe, and then, once it was clear that he would live, trying to fix in his mind that absolute peril, that blankness out beyond the bay. That, he thought, was something he should remember.

69

Penny reckoned that, with the sky lighter, she and George would be safer out in the open. They climbed down the rope from the hayloft and walked up the hill.

The sheep were penned into a small holding area at the top of the clearing. Cyrus stood on the fence rails, shouting and pointing, a still point amid constant motion. The families had gathered, too: Billy Quick and his houseguests, Ann and Barbara, Catta's aunt Diana, Jim and Lila Hillsinger and Isa, but not James nor the Old Man nor Catta. There were other people that Penny did not recognize. Some staff stood at the bottom of the hill, forming a sort of loose funnel to guide the sheep onto the enormous bulwark and then the dock, to land finally on the barge. Some of the Cottage girls were walking up the hill, but no small boys were present. None of their tormentors from last night was anywhere to be seen. Past the houses, at the end of the dock, almost in the center of the harbor itself, she could see the barge waiting.

"Three minutes," Cyrus said, as Penny leaned over the railing.

In that moment, it felt like a festival or a holiday, like the Fourth of July right before the fireworks began. Little Isa Hillsinger dragged her mother and father downhill and others followed, marking out the sheep's path downhill. One farm-hand held Betsy the Border collie by the collar. Cyrus handed a small gun to Billy Quick. Billy pointed the gun up and it went off with a pop. A cheer went up all over the hill. The holding pen swung open. The sheep ran out in a fury.

"Go!" Penny shouted, with all the other children.

She climbed over the railing and ran, and every other child ran, too, a swarm of little feet chasing each other and the sheep down the hill, tripping and falling down and rolling and laughing. Penny ran so fast that she caught the last lamb, who swerved to avoid her. Penny leapt off a rock next to the road and landed in the tall grass, rolled over, and bounced back up and kept running. There was no way to stop—Cyrus thought that all of them, the sheep and the children too, might run blindly into the sea. Betsy the Border collie ran just behind the herd, and at a crucial point she cut through its center, which parted instantly, steering the beasts into the funnel made up of cheering staff. It was like thunder when they reached the planks of the bulwark. The first sheep tried to slow down before stepping onto the barge, apparently afraid of the metal surface, but the rest of the herd was moving fast and pushed all of them back. The barge rail collapsed and two lambs fell off and into the harbor. Betsy then leapt off the dock and paddled after them. She chased them back onto the shore, up the beach, and around the bulwark onto the dock and then the barge again. The staff fixed the battered railing. Order was restored.

Edward Peck pulled the barge away from the dock, waving to the crowd that had gathered. The *Heron* followed. Once the sheep had left, Penny lay on her back in the grass, exhausted, looking up at the early-morning sky. George lay a few feet away. Penny had not known that sheep could swim, and she was sad Catta had not seen the dog save the sheep. She thought he would like George.

"When I find James," George said, "I'm going to hit him."

George stood up and walked toward the Cottage, climbed the front porch steps, and then opened the screen door and let it slam behind him.

"Wait!" she said, but George was already inside. James was older and much bigger. If George really did it, it would be a massacre.

"There you are," she heard James say through the screen door.

Penny opened the door and crossed the hallway to see George running across the living room, about to launch himself across the table at James. It was suicide. None of the small boys was there—Penny thought they must be asleep upstairs.

When George was three yards from the table, James shoved a plate across the table toward him.

"Pancake?" James said with total unconcern, as if last night had not happened and there had never been an Indian Game. "There was only enough batter for one big one."

George stopped himself against a chair and then almost fell over, and Penny finally caught up with him.

"Is there syrup?" Penny said, to fill the silence.

"Just butter," James said.

George sat down at the table. Penny sat down, too, so that they were both across from James. She cut a slab of orange Seven Island butter and spread it out as far as it would go on the one giant pancake, to its very edges. The three of them quietly watched the butter melt.

70

Now Catta was running. Once he got off the beach and onto the forest trails, the rocks and roots cut his bare feet, but he didn't stop until he reached the old lumber camp at Starks Cove, where a two-room shack sat near the dock. Moving quickly, he picked up all the birch bark he could carry and stacked it at the end of the long dock. He went back to the shack and took an oar from a shelf above one of the bunks and laid that on top of the bark. That ended his obligation to North Island.

Now he would have to figure out whether and how to reveal himself. He wanted them to search for him, to fail, to drag the harbors and call the Coast Guard. He wanted them to panic, for his father's eternal calm to vanish. How long would he make them suffer? Dinnertime tonight at the very least, he thought. He could hide out in the barn or in the woods behind the Cottage until it was time to appear, but he would need warm clothes, food, maybe a blanket. Chances were that he would only find a few old horse blankets in the barn, but that was the safest option. He needed something to wear that was not in tatters, and there were always random shirts and pants and sweaters hanging on the hooks in the front hallway of the Cottage. If he scouted the house well, he could be in and out in a few seconds and have everything he needed.

The sun was high. Soon people would be on the trails, so Catta ran. He felt lighter and faster now, almost like he could run for days. He went up and down a stone staircase and through an ugly stretch of cleared timber. The splinters cut his feet, which meant they were too soft. He would never wear shoes again. He crossed one of the big hay fields, not yet cut, and wet green buds stuck to his legs. He ran down the soft path covered over with moss like an emerald tunnel. He passed the ice pond, which lay close to the road, and then the fairy houses, and he hoped Isa had not dragged his mother out there before breakfast. He ran silently, bowed down, close to the ground, hands by his knees, like he imagined the Micmac to have run. The Old Man had said the ice pond was bottomless—Catta wanted to dive in and bring him back a handful of weeds. *Had there been*, he wondered, *an eagles' nest on Baffin after all? Did I miss it?* He came out of the woods on the edge of the uphill pasture, by the graveyard. The high point of the clearing. The two houses and the big barn lay in front of him, and then lower down was the Cottage, the dock, and the ocean.

Catta reckoned the barn would be empty—Sheila would be on North with the rest of the staff. From the hayloft he could see both the Cottage and the Hill House and everything else happening in the clearing. He could evaluate his options from there. The problem was his route. It was safest to take the longer but most concealed path to the barn, so he headed away from the houses and the barn, down the hill to the back fields where the cows had bells, over the fences, and then into the small woods by the ocean. When he arrived at the barn by that back route, he had traveled more than a mile in a wide circle rather than cross a few hundred yards of open ground.

The barn was dark.

"Who's there?" Sheila said, sharply.

Catta walked farther in and turned the corner. Sheila was there kneeling by the Border collie's box, holding a bottle of milk for the little gray body lying among the eight black-and-white puppies.

"You came back," Sheila said.

71

The New House kitchen was in pieces on the floor. Christopher Templeton, who did not cook, had risen early and decided that, with the staff absent for the Migration, he would make the entire house a full lumberjack's breakfast. He pulled everything out of the drawers and cabinets while overlooking the most obvious well-used frying pans that hung unobtrusively from the ceiling. The kitchen was unusable.

Billy Quick considered taking everyone down to the Cottage, where Martha had stockpiled food for the Migration period, but he decided it was too early to deal with children. An outdoor cooking fire was ruled out due to the drought restrictions. It was distasteful and somewhat embarrassing, but begging for breakfast at the Hill House seemed like the best of a bad set of options.

Which was how, when Jim Hillsinger came in from an early walk, he found the entire New House around the oak table in the Hill House dining room. *Twelve hours of independence should not be so hard for them to sustain*, he thought. And yet here they were, enjoying breakfast and a fire (presumably lit by Billy) in the dining room fireplace that, as a matter of policy, was never lit before dinner. Hillsinger managed the pleasantries and even a joke, and Christopher Templeton said that Lila was hard at work in the kitchen.

Hillsinger passed through the two sets of swinging doors and found his wife negotiating multiple pans on the stovetop. The kitchen smelled like coffee and bacon and warm butter.

"Can I help?" he said.

"You may not," Lila said. "You may, however, sit down and entertain our guests, who are somehow victims of the Migration."

"How, exactly?" he said.

"The details are mysterious," Lila said, and Jim went back through the swinging doors.

Thirty minutes before, Lila had been cracking eggs when Billy Quick appeared at the kitchen door, looking mortified. He was at the head of a gang. He must have explained why they were there. She couldn't be sure—she had not been listening.

It has taken, Lila thought. She could tell, even through the screen door. He had noticed. Her capitulation would still be, for Billy, an advanced theory rather than knowledge, but she saw a new hesitation, a slight leaning forward. He wanted confirmation.

There is no conceivable book, Lila thought, for what comes next. She was in some form of love with Billy Quick—and also with her husband and her children and the life they had made. She loved this velocity, and she loved that stasis. She would choose *and* instead of *or*, and *all* instead of *one*. She had walked over the horizon.

"I'm so sorry to hear it," Lila said when Billy finished talking, presumably about the New House kitchen. He had noticed. He was searching. And then she laughed, for the first time in a thousand years.

72

George said he had to find someone named Billy Quick. His aunt had instructed him to do this the minute he set foot on Seven Island, and he was worried it might be seen as rude that he had waited this long, until the morning after his arrival. Penny said she would go with him to the New House and introduce him to her uncle.

Uphill, the New House was quiet. No one responded to Penny's knock. No one was visible through the windows. Only the Hill House showed signs of life. As a recently declared enemy of the Hillsingers, Penny would never have walked alone into the Hill House dining room alone, but now George opened the heavy front door and stepped inside. Penny followed, expecting to flee. A crescendo of adult laughter rose up and fell away.

The two children appeared at the dining room door just as Jim Hillsinger returned from the kitchen. Everyone turned toward them. Hillsinger had never seen the boy before.

"Good morning," this new boy said in a strangely declamatory style, Hillsinger thought, as if he were reciting the Pledge of Allegiance. "Would you please tell me where I could find Billy Quick?"

The adults laughed.

"Not a word until your lawyer wakes up," Christopher Templeton said to Billy, prompting another burst of laughter.

"You must be George," Billy said. "Have a seat."

George began to speak, but Billy stopped him.

"Eat first," he said. The less these children said here in this house, Billy thought, the better for everyone.

Penny kept watch on Jim Hillsinger. He never looked at her directly, or only briefly, and she was relieved when the room's attention shifted and the murmur of adult talk started again. Lila Hillsinger came in from the kitchen to bring them enormous plates of eggs, bacon, more pancakes, even coffee. Although Mrs. Hillsinger rubbed her back gently and asked how her father was, Penny was intensely aware of the exits. She was coiled and ready to run. And then the devil spoke.

"So, George," Jim Hillsinger said, "how was your first night on Seven?"

Don't answer, Penny thought. *It's a trick.*

As far as George was concerned, this morning was much more promising than last night. This, finally, resembled the past three weeks: calm adult voices and food on china plates, followed by laughably simple questions. He was especially glad not to be in a room with James Hillsinger.

Penny, however, imagined all the different and equally bad ways that George could answer that question: *Your son tried to kill me*, he could say, or *I slept in a barn*. She set her legs against the table so she could vault back and run for the woods. If George made them angry, they might come for her first.

"This is the nicest place I've ever been," George said.

"That's a good answer," Jim Hillsinger said.

The adults all laughed, and Penny collapsed against the hard wooden back of her chair.

George had said that exact phrase many times over the last three weeks, about several different places. It was perfect: it ended these dull interrogations in a way that made adults happy enough that they continued to bring him plates of food, and then every few days they took him to a new place. He did not know how long this sort of mystical conveyance would last, but he planned to keep saying it until it no longer worked, or until someone took him home again. The woman whom Billy Quick called *Lila* placed a smaller plate in front of him. She asked him if he liked smoked salmon, and he said yes.

"Thank you, Lila," Billy Quick said as she retreated through the swinging doors.

Back in the kitchen, Lila ransacked the refrigerator and the shelves for other plausible food to bring out, hoping that when she did, Billy Quick would say her name that same way just one more time.

73

In the barn, Catta climbed into the wheelbarrow, and Sheila covered him with a horse blanket. She opened one of the barn's big loading doors and pushed the wheelbarrow over the stretch of grass to the Hill House basement door. She walked past Billy Quick and his guests, who—Sheila whispered—were for some reason all standing at the kitchen door of the wrong house.

"I'm waving to them," Sheila said. "They're waving back."

When Catta saw Sheila, he had not felt anything. She had electrified the known world for him over the last two weeks, and yet, when he had walked into the barn, hearing her voice say *Who's there?* was the first time he had thought about her since he went to Baffin. He wondered if the relentlessness of Baffin had made him unfit for civilization.

"What did you see there?" Sheila said.

"So many trees," he said.

The Hill House basement had endless nooks and hiding places where he could wait while he listened to what was happening upstairs. Sheila had told him that the Old Man was sick, that he had not been down since they'd come back from Baffin, and that made Catta want to see him. Knowing about Baffin would cure his grandfather immediately.

"We're at the basement door," Sheila said. "Everyone is gone."

Catta was out of the wheelbarrow and through the basement door much faster than Sheila would have thought possible. She'd hoped he would turn around or at least look at her briefly before he disappeared, but instead he was up and gone almost in one motion, without turning. She never saw his face. It was not that she wanted him to thank her or even to acknowledge her insignificant presence, but rather that she had something vital to tell him, something that she could not say out loud. This thing would be easier to communicate if she could see his eyes.

"Look," Sheila whispered. "God sent you a wheelbarrow."

74

May 1964
Georgetown, Washington, D.C.

*That Wise Men panel, Forrest said, was not—I repeat, was not—
meant to assess the legitimacy of Subotin. That was a false flag. Its
purpose was to decide the fate of Jim Hillsinger.*

Me? Hillsinger said. It was three days of Subotin talking.

*The decision about Subotin was made months ago, Forrest said.
Angleton said he's dirty, and anyone arguing for him is dirty, too.*

*Hillsinger could feel the horror coming on, but it had not arrived yet.
There was a yellow Counterintelligence sticker on his personnel file.*

*At the beginning of that panel, Forrest continued, you read the faked
Astrakhov material but Danziger and Todd read the Counterintelligence
memo about you.*

Which says what? Hillsinger said.

*Two important things, Forrest said. One is your role in managing
Hannah Quick's escape from the New York Board of Education's witch
hunt in 1955, and the other is your relationship with Hans Kallenbach.*

I have no relationship with Kallenbach.

*Understand, Forrest said, that everything I tell you has been docu-
mented by Counterintelligence. The facts are not in dispute, only their
interpretation. They have a telephone transcript of Kallenbach identify-
ing himself to your wife, apologizing for calling the wrong number, and
hanging up. She seems to know him. She says, and I quote, "Oh, hello,
Hans." To Counterintelligence, that exchange looks like a prearranged
request for a meeting.*

They tapped our phone, too? Hillsinger said.

Everything, Forrest said. The complete package.

The horror now arrived: they had cornered him. Counterintelligence had been immensely thorough, although also wrong. Hillsinger's choices were to trust Forrest completely or to flee, and he was not set up to flee. His only real option was surrender.

I told Peregrine Wilkie, Hillsinger said. I understand that he intervened via a third party.

That's a tough one, Forrest said. It's a predator's law, and she was your sister-in-law. Your bad luck was that Bobby Sheppard defected and then Angleton took out his microscope on the Harlem teachers and, when pressed, your FBI contact rolled on you. Suddenly the extenuating circumstances didn't matter. Now Jim Hillsinger is a high CIA official who kept a known associate of a defector out of jail, out of the papers, whatever. Angleton was incensed. Hence the surveillance and your phone tap, which in turn generated Kallenbach. I would not, by the way, tell your wife about this. The less she knows, the better I can protect her.

It is strange, Hillsinger said, that Lila seemed to know him.

You never met him socially?

No.

Angleton agreed, Forrest said, that both the Hannah Quick and Kallenbach things are arguably minor in and of themselves, but that they were actionable if part of a larger pattern. The Director suggested this Wise Men panel as a tiebreaker.

I was right about Subotin, Hillsinger said.

From the Counterintelligence point of view, Forrest said, you had multiple chances to make the correct decision—to reject someone they believe is clearly a KGB provocation. They showed you a version of the Astrakhov material, you saw Subotin himself get everything wrong, Danziger and Todd explicitly laid out the case for the prosecution, and, to judge by the transcript, Danziger even tried to bully you into safety.

Do you believe a real penetration exists? Hillsinger said.

Yes, Forrest said.

Then why am I not in jail?

The vote, Forrest said. The poll at the end was about you, not Subotin. Danziger voted No—meaning that you are guilty of treason—and Todd, as you know, voted Inconclusive.

Why was Todd Inconclusive?

Something you said at the end, apparently.

So it was a split, Hillsinger said.

Hung jury, Forrest said. The Director gave Counterintelligence a vote. Their vote was always going to be guilty, so to balance that, he gave me a vote, too.

You.

Me.

That's why you've seen the transcripts.

Correct.

Have you already decided, Hillsinger said, or is your vote contingent on this meeting?

It's done, Forrest said.

And?

I said Inconclusive.

Do you think I'm lying?

Politically, Forrest said, it was the only way I could maintain enough credibility to be able to broker something.

So I'm already gone, Hillsinger said.

Let me ask you for the record: are you a traitor?

No, Hillsinger said.

That's what I told the Director, Forrest said. Counterintelligence wants you in the cell next to Subotin, but they don't have enough to prosecute. So instead, a graceful exit.

How graceful? Hillsinger said.

You will be offered the open post of Station Chief in Pretoria. You will decline this offer, citing family issues. After a short and tasteful interval, lasting no longer than a week, you will resign without pension. That, the pension, was Angleton's condition. Allen Dulles is talking to people about a job for you, but either way you'll have to leave Washington.

Pretoria, Hillsinger said.

It was the best I could do on short notice, Forrest said.

75

Catta stood in the basement. A roar broke the general hum coming from the floor above, before it died away and chairs squeaked, someone spoke, people laughed. Someone spoke. At one point he was sure he heard his mother and then she laughed, and he was furious—of all people, she should never laugh until he was back home. Slowly the collective noise built back up to the point where all the voices were once again indistinguishable.

The basement seemed larger than the house: he found a set of ancient refrigerators, racks of wine, abandoned bathtubs and toilets, and a row of children's boots by the door. He was certain that his grandfather would want to know about the ravine on Baffin and the spring, *which meant that owls were here*, or at least it meant that they could be. And if his grandfather exposed him—if he raised an alarm, or called his father—then Catta would know that the adults in the family were corrupt beyond any possibility of hope. Dale and Conrad had said exactly that, and it was worth any amount of risk to know such a big thing for sure.

Once he'd made a full circuit of the huge basement, Catta began to understand which parts of it corresponded to which rooms overhead. He figured out what the oddly shaped door was in the main hallway upstairs. It was smaller than the other ones and rounded at the top instead of square. That door opened opposite the back stairs to the second floor.

Catta climbed the narrow stairs, which creaked. He stood behind the door, among the cobwebs, listening to his own amplified breathing. He waited for a sign. There was a burst of laughter. *That was it*—he opened the door. No one was there. He stood in the open for a brief second, glorying in the starkness of his contempt, and then opened the door to the back staircase and climbed it with quick feet.

Catta had never been in the second-floor hallway before. The rules on Seven were complex, and one of them was that children could never go upstairs in the Hill House. The hallway was quiet; all sound was swallowed by the heavy red carpet, and all the doors were closed. He had no idea which room was his grandfather's, so he walked the length of the hall and saw only one door with any sign of life—a plate, sitting on a tray, with crumbs and a crust of yolk. The door was locked.

"Go away!" the Old Man said.

Catta knocked softly, three times.

"I've had my breakfast. Go away!"

Catta knocked yet again—light, calm, persistent, as if the knocking would never stop. He heard rustling, and then the lock clicked and the door swung open.

The Old Man, who normally wore a blazer even in hot weather, was in pajamas and a battered robe. His mouth was open in the act of screaming, but his voice and his whole body froze when he saw Catta, who held a finger to his lips. The Old Man slowly retreated into the dim room, where the blinds were drawn, and sat down on his single bed. Catta stepped inside, shut the door, and leaned against it. It was hard to see in there, though eventually he could make out a wooden chair in the corner. He crossed to it and sat down. He had expected the Old Man to speak, to demand answers or even ring his bell, but his grandfather said nothing and did not move. He was hunched over, facing the door, his head only partway visible.

"There's a spring on Baffin," Catta said after a long silence.

The Old Man considered this for longer than seemed normal. He did not meet Catta's eye.

"I came back to tell you," Catta said.

The risk was that the first thing his grandfather might do with the information would be to commandeer a boat and go to Baffin to see for himself—so Catta added, quickly: "I could never find it again. It was just luck that I found it at all."

The Old Man looked at the window as if the blinds were open, although they were not.

"Were there owls?" the Old Man said.

"Yes," Catta said. "I saw one for just a second, and then it was gone."

There might have been, Catta thought, a thousand owls on Baffin. It had been so dark that he could not see anything at all. But he could do this small thing for his grandfather—for the Old Man, distant springs equaled owls. That had been his theory for Catta's whole life. He could carry his logic through to the end.

"What color?" his grandfather said.

"Gray," Catta said, "with white tips on its wings."

"Gray with white tips," his grandfather repeated.

The Old Man climbed under the bedcovers. Catta wanted to ask his grandfather to keep his presence secret, but he felt as if speaking now were out of place. He was embarrassed—it seemed imposing and possibly improper to stay in the room while his grandfather was in bed, as if sleep in so old a man was somehow indecent. Catta crossed back to the door and left.

As it happened, the Old Man was overwhelmed equally by his most recent illness, which had started yesterday, on the boat, and by the resonance of Catta's information. At Château-Thierry, in what they now called the First World War, there were ten owls in each abandoned barn. On the same day that the order came for them to go over the trenches, he had woken up with a dual premonition: first, that he would survive the fighting that day, which as it turned out was a horrific bloodbath, and second, that owls would in some way figure prominently in his fate. The second half of his vision was obviously preposterous, and yet his escape that day had been so narrow—so many others had died—that in this sense, the owls were tied inextricably to his own salvation. As a boy, he had seen two white ones in the Adirondacks, and then the multitude in France and Germany during the war. Never since then, though, and never here on Seven, which for him was the only place that really mattered. But he was willing to wait, and, since the appearance of owls had been both predicted and in a larger sense preordained, the reality was that every day when he did *not* see an owl was also a day when it was impossible for him to die.

This was relevant because, lately, he had begun to have these shocks. He did not consider them to be a disease since they went away quickly (although they came back). He had no acute symptoms. No bleeding or unbearable pain. The doctors had seen nothing. He would, however, grow suddenly weak: fever-ish, intensely hungry, only in the morning and only for eggs. The shocks had grown more frequent; the membrane between life and death seemed to him especially thin. He could now hear, every day, the valediction of the sun. He had consulted his more farsighted friends, including Peregrine Wilkie, who argued that they must reject the temptations of passivity. He often spoke like that, Peregrine did, as if he were at the head of an army, and a thousand men stood in the shadows behind him. At a certain point, Peregrine said—at a point which was unknowable, until it was not—they must find the will to walk cheerfully into the gathering storm.

His grandson had filtered in and out of the Old Man's half-sleep ever since they'd returned from Baffin, but this last vision of Catta, his torso covered in cuts and slashes and with a strange mark on its left shoulder, clearly a seven, had made him suspect delirium. It was possible, he concluded, and even likely that his body was strangling his mind. The apparition's talk of owls confirmed it. He could not approach this great reckoning in a state of dementia and fog. He must act, insofar as he could.

As he unfolded the heavy woolen blanket back over himself, the Old Man saw at last, like mist burning off to reveal a mountain range nearby, that the deeper meaning of the owls' long absence had been simply this: to certify the truth of a messenger who would come to announce his moment of decision. This effigy of Catta was that messenger. He stacked the books, tidied his bedsheets, swept the night table items into a drawer, and embraced the pseudo-Catta's message in the same spirit of ferocity with which he had lived.

He died three hours later, in relative peace, with an obscure verse of "The Battle Hymn of the Republic" echoing through his head.

76

When he left the Old Man's room, after telling him about the owls, Catta had retreated to the basement. He stood by the outside door and realized that he was effectively trapped. He could not get back to the tree line, or even the barn, without being seen from the Hill House windows. Sheila had, however, left behind the wheelbarrow that brought him from the barn. And here, hanging by the door, was a large bright-yellow foul-weather coat. Firewood lay piled by the door. Catta reckoned that anyone looking out the window who saw someone pushing a wheelbarrow full of logs while wearing a raincoat on a beautiful day would assume some staff member had been left behind from the Migration for unknown reasons. No questions would be asked. The real danger was meeting someone between here and the barn, so he had to move fast, before the breakfast window closed.

It worked: he did not see anyone and no one called out to him. Colt was sleeping, and Sheila was not in the barn. Catta took off the absurd rain gear and laid it carefully on one of the stalls. He climbed up to the hayloft to scout the clearing.

Catta approached the Cottage from the rear, from the woods. There was no movement inside the house, but every ten yards he stopped and waited, to make sure he could not be seen. It was still early enough that the small boys would be asleep if they were lazy, which they usually were, and Martha was gone for the Migration so nobody would wake the stragglers. Martha would have left long trays of food in the refrigerator with precise instructions for heating them up, all of which would be ignored—the kids would eat everything cold. Catta could fill up a bag with food and be set for the day and the night, too, if it came to that.

When he got close to the Cottage, he looked in each window. No one was awake or around. Then he was in the front hallway. He stopped to listen. Everything was quiet. Different boys' clothes were on hooks in the hallway, and he felt more human when he put a shirt on his back and a sweater, too.

He was through the hardest part, he thought. He was more than halfway home. Next was the kitchen—to eat or at least to pack up food for the day, if possible. He walked silently through the living room, pausing for a few seconds to see if the fireplace ashes were still warm. They were not. Then he stepped through the kitchen door into the butler's pantry. His luck, Catta thought, had been good. He had been right to leave Baffin. Now starving, he walked into the kitchen.

And there was James.

He sat on the floor of the kitchen, eating cold pancakes out of a large metal tray. He smiled before he spoke.

"You must be hungry," he said.

Catta turned and ran, but he slipped trying to turn the corner. Behind him, he heard the metal tray slam onto the floor.

James would sell him out to his father right away. Catta's only option now was to throw himself into the Hill House dining room and tell them everything before James made up something horrible, before he told his father all the lies he could think of.

Catta slammed through the screen door and jumped off the porch to the ground. He still did not have shoes on and he was running too slowly, like in a bad dream. Catta heard James just behind him, and then he felt him. James was fast. He swerved but not soon enough, and James hit him across the back of the head. Catta lost his balance and fell down, landing hard on his back, and before he could cover up James punched him in the stomach. For a long time he could not move or breathe, while James ran up the hill to seal his fate. And the cuts on Catta's back were on fire.

77

Lila Hillsinger was carrying a large tray of scrambled eggs and bacon into the dining room when her son James appeared at the head of the table.

"Catta's here!" James shouted.

No one spoke. For her own self-preservation, Lila could not even hope that it was true—James had a history of indiscretion, even outright lies.

"Please explain yourself," Jim said.

"He's out there," James said, pointing toward the lawn. "He ran away, but I can find him."

Since Lila could not yet commit to believing it, she was able to bend over and gently place the china tray safely on the table. When she straightened up again, Catta had appeared behind James.

"Look!" James said. "He was afraid and he came home."

Catta had been terrified of James's relentless prosecution, of his lies, of everything. And yet James sounded absolutely ridiculous in this room, with his empty words exposed to the air.

Lila moved across the room and tried to embrace Catta, but he jumped back before she could touch him.

"What?" Lila said, now recoiling, almost falling over backward.

Under the borrowed shirt, Catta's back was a patchwork of raw cuts, but he did not want to say that. Just now, any form of speaking felt like a lie. He didn't know what to do.

"Look at his feet," Wilkie said to Billy in his secret voice.

"Catta," Billy said, "what happened to your feet?"

At first, Lila was irritated that Billy had spoken—it was not his place. But then she saw Catta's feet. Everything was cut and scratched, and what was not cut or scratched was caked in blood.

"Did you come all the way back here barefoot?" Billy continued.

Wilkie was surprised by Catta's silence. It was obviously true—why wouldn't he say it?

Catta looked at the variety of surprised or confused adult faces. Maybe, he thought, the answer was just to lie: it seemed like what they wanted.

"Catta," Jim Hillsinger said, "take off your shirt."

When he'd obeyed this request, Wilkie turned to Lila. She looked like someone watching a body fall from high up in the air.

She was confused when Catta had jumped back from her touch, but still delighted—anything was fine with her, any reaction at all, so long as he was safe inside this house. And then she saw what had happened to his body. The cuts that almost looked like lashes, the blood.

"Turn around, darling," Lila said.

If anything, his back was worse. For Lila, the most damning detail was that *he had done this to himself*. Jim had put him on an island, on its shoreline. Presumably he could have waited out his time there. But he had not waited, or he'd been forced to go inland on an island with notoriously impassable vegetation. And Catta had not merely done that, taken that rather extreme step, but then he had *persisted* in the face of this obvious pain. What would make a boy of twelve do that? In what sort of world was

245

it even possible? Their house was not a place of safety, as she had thought. It was a coliseum.

And if that was true, if her marriage was not a partnership but a proving ground, or a stall for breeding violent oxen, then what was the rest of it? What was the meeting in Philadelphia, the ascending arc of intimacy, the unspoken knowledge—was that all just prelude to the sacrifice of warriors? Was the flaying of her younger son what her husband had meant when he spoke about his work on *the psychological front*? Had Lila in the end *not* been nurturing her children, as she had believed—had she instead been fattening them up for slaughter?

"This is a surprise," Jim said to Catta. "Why don't you tell us what happened?"

"The real surprise here," Billy said in what Lila thought was more her sister's old register of self-righteousness, "is that you almost killed your son."

"Thank you, Billy, for your usual penetration," Jim said, without looking at him. "Catta, I want you to listen carefully."

"I'm listening," Catta said.

"Understand that if I were trying to kill you, you would be dead."

Wilkie nearly laughed out loud. Hillsinger had posed an impossible question to his son, and against the odds Catta had answered it correctly. The question was, by Wilkie's lights, a variant of *Tell me something I don't already know*. And the answer was here in front of him, it was written all over Catta's back, legs, feet, and torso, and it seemed—astonishingly, for Wilkie— that Hillsinger was delighted. Wilkie reckoned that if Catta had built a ziggurat from stones, or captured a songbird with a string and two worms, Hillsinger would have been almost equally pleased. He had wanted Catta to do something unexpected, something *virtuosic*. The contrast here between him and Lila was stark.

"Darling," Lila said to Catta, "put your shirt back on."

Before he did put his shirt on, before she turned away, Lila noticed what looked like a number 7 there on his upper arm. What could that possibly be? Her son had come back from Baffin a stranger.

When James Hillsinger saw that Catta would not be punished or humiliated or sent back to Baffin, he left the room and the Hill House. They'd fooled him again.

He went into the barn to see if the staff had left the little lamb-dog behind, when they left for the Migration. The other boys had loved seeing it the other night, and even if Sheila had stayed behind, too, James thought he could convince her to let him take it down to the Cottage for an hour. At worst, she would let them all come up to see it later in the day. As it happened, though, when James went in, Sheila was asleep next to the Border collie's box, with its freight of newborn dogs and the one gray lamb.

There was an orange bucket hanging by the birthing-pen. James took the bucket down and placed it next to the box, and then, with infinite care, he picked up the tiny lamb in both hands and slid him into the bucket. He was so gentle that the lamb kept sleeping.

There was an odd, almost imploring silence, Wilkie thought, while the boy ate. Jim Hillsinger, who sat close to Catta but not next to him, remained completely still, while Billy Quick changed position every few minutes, crossing and uncrossing. All the other adults were quiet. Lila hovered and ran relays into the kitchen, bringing out more and more food that, once his first wave of hunger had passed, Catta no longer wanted.

"How did you get across?" Billy finally said. "I've tried to walk in from the beach and I couldn't go more than a few feet."

"I got small," Catta said. "Most of the branches either don't go all the way to the ground or, if they do, they don't extend too high."

Penny Quick, meanwhile, had been laughing quietly ever since Catta sat down. Wilkie could not imagine why, but Catta seemed to appreciate it. When he smiled for the first time, it was in her direction. George, the new boy, looked completely lost. *What an introduction*, Wilkie thought.

"How did you get off the island?" Hillsinger said.

That question silenced the room. It seemed to Wilkie that even the dense ones, like Christopher Templeton, recognized that this was the crucial question—even with his body punished, as it had been, even if he had in fact successfully crossed the island in the dark—even granting all these feats, *if* (for example) Catta had been picked up by a passing lobster boat or found a canoe by chance, then that would change the complexion of the thing entirely, and for the worse. Yet Hillsinger's tone continued to be light. Wilkie reflected that he was a professional interrogator who would have routinely confronted dangerous men with at least the implied threat of violence. It was both remarkable and terrifying to see Hillsinger deploy skills he used against the KGB in questioning a twelve-year-old boy.

"I swam," Catta said, precisely matching Hillsinger's unconcerned tone.

"You swam the fast channel?" Billy Quick said.

"Yes," Catta said.

"What time did you leave Baffin?" Jim Hillsinger said.

Hillsinger did not quite believe it, Wilkie thought. He wanted to believe it, but he was trying to rule out his own worst hypothesis—that the boy was just making it all up. Hillsinger must have a good idea of what time high tide was, Wilkie reckoned, and therefore he knew how fast, how dangerously, and in what direction the water would have been moving through that channel at any particular time.

"I woke up at dawn and left right after," Catta said.

"Where did you land on Seven?" Billy said.

"The Long Beach."

"From Baffin to the Long Beach is a long way to swim."

"The current was fast. I thought it was going to take me out into the ocean, but in the bay it slowed down and then just dropped off, and I swam for it. I was lucky. The water's cold there. It's much colder than the harbor."

At that, Lila left the room. Hillsinger watched her go.

"The tattoo," Hillsinger said, turning back to Catta.

"I used the fish hook I brought with me," Catta said. "And a squid washed up on the beach still had its ink sac. I don't know if it'll last."

They would never believe him about the squid, but it didn't matter. He was sure the tattoo would last.

"By the way," Catta said to his father, almost too casually, as if he were telling him the time, "there are owls on Baffin."

80

Down in the orange bucket, the lamb was making feeble suck-ing sounds that James did not like. He'd rallied the small boys, and they were hiking to the usual meeting place in the woods behind the Cottage. James walked behind the rest of them—they didn't know he was bringing something special, and James wanted to produce an effect. The boys were astonished when he pulled the lamb from the bucket, even the ones who had seen it before. James fed it some milk from the kitchen, with a spoon, and each boy took a turn holding it. One of them asked James what Sheila had said when he took the lamb away.

"It's the Migration," James said. "Whoever the staff leaves behind is cut off. This lamb is sick. He's in pain."

The small boys were silent. None of them knew what sickness looked like in animals, certainly not in sheep. One of the Templeton boys had seen Sheila just twenty minutes ago through the bunk room window. She had been running frantically along the tree line back behind the Cottage, calling out for Colt. At the time, the boy thought, it had seemed ridiculous.

James asked them: did they want to be part of something important—something extraordinary? They did. Did they believe, James asked, in the supremacy of kindness? Heads nodded. And did they believe animals had souls, that a lamb too would ultimately live forever? Murmuring. *Yes.*

Holding the orange bucket in one hand, James led the boys in a line through the forest to the shoreline, and then around two headlands to the empty Seven dock. The clearing was empty. It was low tide, and the seaweed was exposed on the rocks. James walked into Cyrus's workshop and cut a long piece of twine. Out on the dock a flat stone weighed down the top of the floating lobster pen, and James tied one end of the twine to that stone. He wrapped the other end around the lamb's belly and knotted it before putting both lamb and stone back into the bucket.

"This is the only way," James said to the boys, and he emptied the orange bucket into the harbor.

81

Sheila was confused. It was bright inside the barn and the angle of the sun was higher and there was a copper taste in her mouth. She must have been asleep, which was bad. It was a miracle that anything or anyone survived infancy.

When she looked down, eight black-and-white puppies were lined up in a row, sleeping. All was well. Her second thought was that the anomaly was missing. She could not see Colt. Sheila stood up and shook her head and turned around to remove any sleep-related blindness. She counted to ten. She looked down again. Colt was still gone.

There were so few options: someone might have taken him, but the staff and Betsy were all gone to North Island. Something feral might have grabbed him, but why him and not a puppy? There were barn cats and possums, but they did not normally attack anything in the barn. Colt could not crawl out on his own. She had been afraid enough of all these possibilities to stay awake for hours at a time, but she also believed that her vigilance itself was a strong talisman that would keep those threats away. Cyrus would not have approved of either her actions or her thinking, but that was what she believed. It had protected all of them so far.

She avoided the thought of retribution—the idea that the taking of Colt was the result of her refusal to go to North herself, or to allow him to go. That this was damnation. Cyrus would say her offense was *mysticism*, what he called the belief that any one person's experience was more essential, more enlightened, or more direct than that of the congregation as a whole.

Sheila went through each part of the barn in widening circles, lifting everything that moved: saddles, tools, blankets, anything within ten yards of Betsy's box. She searched farther and farther out, in all the stalls and closets and upstairs in the hayloft where Penny and George had slept. There was no Colt. With rising panic, she walked and then ran along the tree line by the barn, lifting branches and running her hand through shrubs, calling out for Colt although she knew he couldn't speak.

82

Since her marriage Lila had, for reasons she did not fully understand, let lapse the talent for self-laceration that had marked so
much of her youth. When they met she had been overwhelmed
by the sense of being *chosen*, not by Jim necessarily although
that, too, but rather by some larger, deeper, more transformative
logic. *What luck*, she had thought then. More than luck, really,
—*What luminous signs*, she'd thought. Emboldened, Lila had—
she and Jim had, both separately and together—set out toward a
life lived at a scale and intensity equal to their omens. At that
time, in New York and Washington, with the rising Soviet
threat, the CIA had seemed to answer that extravagant demand.

But now this other thing came flooding back. This excava-
tion of herself, of what she had done and still hoped to do: now
she was again the Lila Blackwell who, in the long-ago days when
she had worn a white coat to church, had been loved so often
from afar. The contradiction was intoxicating.

Across the lawn, Sheila was shouting into the tall grass.

Lila could not comfort or heal Catta as she was now—afraid
to touch him, afraid that he was irretrievably changed, afraid that
Jim might have been right to send him—so she walked toward
the sad girl and was startled to hear her calling "Colt! Colt!
Colt!" in all directions, as if the little lamb were playing
hide-and-seek.

"Sheila!" Lila said.

Now the poor girl was crying uncontrollably. She could not
speak except to say *Colt*.

"How long has he been missing?" Lila said.

"An hour," she said.

"Let's get help," Lila said, and Sheila nodded in the empty way that one accepts one's doom.

Lila ran down the hill to the Cottage, where James and the small boys were laughing around the table. She explained the situation: the small lamb had gone missing, and they must search the clearing from top to bottom. James jumped up and said that he would help—they all would help. How terrible for Sheila, James said. He assigned each boy a sector of the clearing and said he should search it and report back in thirty minutes.

The boys scattered all over, calling out for Colt. The show of force and solidarity seemed to improve Sheila's spirits. That was something. Diana and Billy and the Templetons and Isa all eventually joined the search, and then the staff joined, too, when they came back on boats and barges from the Migration. They found a wallet and two arrowheads, but not the lamb. Sheila was inconsolable. The girl cried in Lila's arms for more than an hour.

83

They found the Old Man's body early that evening, when the nurse from the mainland came to take his blood pressure. His will, which lay on his night-table in a manila envelope, was fantastically detailed, listing more than two hundred separate items to be disbursed: books, lighters, ashtrays, cuff links. It specified a service in the Seven chapel followed by burial in the graveyard here alongside his wife. Lila decided that they would tell the children tomorrow rather than tonight. She thought the news would be less of a shock to them, especially to Isa, if they heard it when the sun was out.

That night, Lila slept in her own bed. She fell effortlessly into the warmth of her duties as the mourner's wife, and it was a relief to have those decisions ready-made. Arrange for more food than necessary. Hug the children. Et cetera. If she owed Jim anything apart from her public role—one that she had executed to perfection—then it was simply to be present. And here she was. Meanwhile, the larger struggle raged inside her— the war between her body and her mind over Billy Quick. Surprisingly, Lila slept well.

She woke to the sunrise breaking over Jim's left shoulder. The night before she had fallen asleep convinced that something in her was diseased and the diseased part must be removed. This morning was different. She was not only optimistic—*she was ecstatic.*

It had taken Lila much too long, she thought, to see the world clearly. It had been hidden from her that she was a born traitor, built to live out some brutal paradox at its farthest possible reach. But now she was home.

84

That afternoon, Lila and Jim went down to the chapel. They sat on the benches next to the water, hand in hand, among the bees. Neither spoke for a long time.

In that prismatic silence, Lila had this one thought: that life lay in a gamble that her heart was vast enough to hold two truths so radically opposed. On the one hand, the solidity and warmth of her existing life. On the other, the velocity she now felt when confronted with Billy Quick, another, darker variant of the truth. Both were necessary; to abandon either would be a catastrophic loss.

"What about Billy?" Lila said, and the hummingbirds scattered.

Jim paused for a long time.

"What do you want?" he said.

All that was left was for Lila to choose. She would not. Instead, she would lie to the worst possible man for her to lie to—the man who knew her so well, who told and spotted lies for a living.

"I want to destroy him," Lila said.

"Define *destroy*."

"I want him," Lila said, "to have a long period of active and painful distress. I want all of his endeavors to fail. Whatever is just short of shooting himself in the head, and that only for the sake of the girls."

"Why not," Jim said, "just leave it alone?"

Her path was narrow here. If the response was either too enthusiastic or too clinical, then Jim, with his infinite subtlety, would immediately see the truth, which was that very public hatred was the best way to hide the obscenity of her true path.

"He hurt us," Lila said. "I allowed him to hurt us."

It felt wrong even when she said it. It was a false note—but then again, the world is full of dissonance. What would he say? Had he seen through her? She couldn't look at him. It was not outlandish to hope that desperation had made her credible.

"It's possible," Jim said. "But we'd have to get Kallenbach first."

It's working, Lila thought. She and Jim would be partners and coconspirators in their marriage, as she wanted in the past and wanted still, as the world had so obviously intended. *Millions now living will never die.*

"What do I do?" Lila said, although she knew what his answer would be.

"You won't like it," he said.

Lila said nothing, waiting patiently for him to continue.

"He has to think I sold you to him."

"Billy would?" Lila said.

"Yes."

Now Lila was laughing.

"Do it," she said. "Do anything you can think of."

85

"What did you learn?" his father said to Catta that night after dinner.

They sat in two chairs in the Old Man's study, in front of the empty desk. His father had not offered him whiskey, but he did give him two things: his grandfather's binoculars, which were in his will, and an old green leather copy of the *Crito*, which was not. The book was printed in both Greek and English.

"I learned how to cross Baffin," Catta said.

He knew that was not the answer, or the type of answer, his father was looking for. He did not care.

"Could you do it again?" his father said.

"If I had to," Catta said.

"Would you?"

"No," Catta said.

His grandfather's study smelled like leather and old smoke, and what Catta liked most about the room was that its peculiar smell was so strong that, when he walked outside, he was resensitized to the salt air again. It was like finally being able to see colors.

"You don't know this," his father said, "but in my professional life I have spent an inordinate amount of time trying to tell who is telling the truth and who is not, often when the stakes are high, in some cases when the stakes are life and death."

"Why?"

"It was asked of me."

"And what did you learn?" Catta said.

"Some useful things," his father said. "For example: I believe you told the truth about most of what happened on Baffin. I also believe that you lied about some of it."

"You believe," Catta said.

His father smiled. That surprised him.

"Yes," his father said. "I also believe that what you did during that period of time was indisputably brave but also reckless. Both the walking and the swimming—neither was strictly necessary. A cynic might call those choices needlessly elaborate."

"Are you a cynic?" Catta said.

"That's a good question."

Catta liked being in his grandfather's study. He liked that he was summoned, he liked being addressed—if not as an equal, which was impossible—then at least not as a wayward child. He felt the urge to tell his father the precise history of his tattoo and about the men and those transports of the Migration that were so secret the men would only hint at them. But Catta had promised silence in a way that mattered, and then, also, could not speak like his father: in paragraphs, with total clarity, in a way that even a hostile listener—that Conrad himself—would recognize and even approve. Today, for him, being silent conveyed more of the truth than speaking would.

"However," his father continued, "your fabrications actually make me more impressed. To learn when to lie, and to whom, and how to do it well—these are all parts of the world, or at least they are part of the unfortunate world that we have left you. Or so I believe."

"So you believe," Catta said.

"Yes," his father said, smiling. "So I believe."

86

By the next night, Templetons, Kipps, and Van Colls had left on the afternoon ferry, and Billy Quick was finally alone in the New House. Tonight he was cooking dinner for himself in order to think without interruption, to formulate a plan.

There was a knock on the kitchen door, and Billy opened it. He was surprised to see Jim Hillsinger and John Wilkie.

"Let's talk about Hans Kallenbach," Hillsinger said.

Billy was not especially alarmed by the mention of Kallenbach. On the spectrum of dubious things his clients did with their money, giving cash from time to time to a seemingly random assortment of black sheep and actresses and junkies, as Hans did, was not especially conspicuous.

"Do I need my lawyer?" Billy said.

"No," Wilkie said.

"Then come in."

Billy waved at the kitchen table while he himself remained standing, tending to a large steak in a cast-iron pan on the stove. Hillsinger and Wilkie sat at the table. Billy poured them each a glass of wine.

"I can't discuss my clients," Billy said.

"Are you aware," Hillsinger said, "that Hans Kallenbach is a known KGB operative?"

"No, I'm not."

"Have you yourself knowingly been in contact with agents of any foreign governments?"

"John," Billy said, turning to Wilkie, "are you really party to this?"

"A storm is gathering, Billy," Wilkie said.

"I asked John to come with me here today for two reasons," Hillsinger said. "First, Peregrine Wilkie is at risk here. He contributed both the seed money for your current fund and also introductions to several other investors, including Hans Kallenbach. As a result Peregrine is a party to the decisions you are about to make, and since Peregrine is now also my employer, so am I."

"I'm not aware of Hans's activities apart from the money he has with me."

"Second," Hillsinger said, "Wilkie is here to witness our agreement."

"I doubt we're going to agree on much of anything."

Hillsinger smiled. "We shall see," he said. "What are you making?"

"In what sense?" Billy said.

"What are you making for dinner?"

"Steak," Billy said. "Would you like some?"

"No, thank you."

"So the trade is—what?" Billy said.

"Wilkie tells me you have a photographic memory," Hillsinger said.

"He's exaggerating."

"That's a shame," Hillsinger said, "because the trade is that you put down for me, right now, without a signature, the complete list of Kallenbach's third-party payments over the last two years, including names, addresses, and any known aliases."

"In return for?"

"Services rendered," Hillsinger said.

"What services?"

"When you agree to this deal, which you will," Hillsinger continued, "two otherwise inevitable things do *not* happen. First: I do not divorce Lila and publicly name you as the reason. Were that to happen, I can name seven of your twelve largest investors who would withdraw their money from you the next day. Second: I do not put it in the papers that Kallenbach is a Soviet spy and that you are his paymaster. That would take care of the other five. It would also precipitate immediate FBI action against you."

"That would precipitate immediate FBI action against *you*," Billy said.

"Leaks happen all the time."

"Again, Jim—I don't know anything about Hans's work."

"Has he been in your apartment?"

"Yes, of course."

"Has he, for example, ever brought presents for your girls?"

Only now did Billy begin to see the larger picture. Now he was concerned.

"And did you or did you not make cash payments out of Kallenbach's account to people other than Kallenbach?"

"It's not my money," Billy said. "When people ask for it, I give it to them."

"You are intimate with a prominent KGB banker. You distributed cash to his designated representatives, some of whom I am sure will prove to be known operatives of the KGB. From a prosecutor's point of view, there's no ambiguity."

He wanted so much to be angry, but Billy felt only relief. A convoluted set of choices had been reduced to one. He had been wrong the other night, in front of the fire, about Lila. He did not know what Hillsinger's plan was for him, but he knew that there was one, somewhere in the background.

"What will you do with the list?" Billy said.

"I will trade the names to my former employer for certain considerations."

"Such as?"

"Such as ensuring that Peregrine Wilkie is protected from future inquiries into Kallenbach's associates. I also expect our close knowledge of this affair to be a strong selling point for Keene Wilkie's services going forward."

"The Kallenbach affair?" Billy said.

"Correct."

"You've been quiet, John," Billy said, turning to Wilkie. "Where do you stand?"

Billy was aware that *Where do you stand?* was John Wilkie's least-favorite question. Almost pathologically, Wilkie preferred to stand in between parties, especially when strong opinions were opposed. He lived in the middle ground.

"The worst case," Wilkie said, "for my father and the firm, is that you and Kallenbach are *both* prosecuted. Then Peregrine looks like a referral service for Communist spies. For you, for me, for us, I'd prefer that only Kallenbach was in jeopardy. I came here to guarantee the integrity of any deal, not to negotiate it, but what Jim is offering strikes me as the best thing for everyone in this room."

"What about me?" Billy said. "Am I protected?"

"Your chances are better," Hillsinger said. "Dramatically better."

"That's not especially compelling."

"There's already a thick file with your name on it."

"Are you referring to my wife's interrogation?"

"That's part of it. I've seen that file, by the way. And if you want to know who killed Hannah, it was Hans Kallenbach."

"Why is that?"

"Trying to get at him—through you—was the whole reason the FBI were after her."

"Why haven't the FBI asked me themselves?"

"Because your wife killed herself in a bathtub."

Billy's strange feeling of relief returned. All taboo subjects were being raised at once. He almost felt loved.

"The FBI stood down *temporarily*," Wilkie said. "Hannah bought you a short space of time before Kallenbach is cashiered by either the FBI or Moscow. If you don't move in one direction or the other, then you will be indicted as an accomplice."

"Let's assume that's true," Billy said, turning back to Hillsinger. "Why should I deal with you instead of directly with FBI and/ or the CIA?"

"If you go to them naked," Hillsinger said, "they'll automatically assume you're under Kallenbach's control."

"I might take my chances."

Hillsinger laughed.

"For a while there," he said, "both the FBI and CIA thought I was under KGB control because Kallenbach called my house once. What chance do *you* have?"

"Same as you, I expect."

"They know me. More important, they know that you're my wife's lover. They are in the business of understanding leverage."

So, Billy thought, it was all out. He had been grotesquely overmatched all along. What kept him from capitulating right away, though, was the black cloud that had floated in his mind for years—the possibility that Hillsinger had informed on Hannah in the first place. On present evidence, he was more than capable of it.

"Tell me something," Billy said.

"This offer is not negotiable."

"John," Billy said, turning to Wilkie, "who really sent you to us in Harlem in '55? Who told you about the Board of Education summons that time you asked Hannah to resign?"

"If I tell you that," Wilkie said, "do we have a deal?"

"I hesitate," Billy said, "because that same person could also have told the FBI about Hannah's Communist ties in the first place."

"You think I'm playing both sides," Hillsinger said. "Fair enough. The fact is that *I* told Wilkie about the Board of Ed summons."

"You?"

"A contact at the FBI reached out to me, and I called Peregrine."

"That was kind of you," Billy said.

"It wasn't."

"How did they know about her in the first place?"

"Hannah was mentioned," Hillsinger said, "in an informant's report from 1947. However, she had enrolled in the Communist Party under her maiden name and therefore was listed in the reports as Hannah Blackwell. For a time, that protected her because her employment record with the School Board was under Hannah Quick. Remarkably, no one at the FBI made the connection. By the way, the informant who named her, ironically enough, was Bobby Sheppard, now a defector to East Germany but at the time a cartoonist. Later on, famously, he was a substitute teacher at Hannah's school. When Sheppard defected, they reopened all of his old Harlem reports, and the penny dropped."

Billy looked at Hillsinger for a moment. Their entire history suggested that this man was his enemy, but his strongest instinct now was to put himself in Hillsinger's hands. Billy took a note-book and pen from a drawer, and sat down at the table.

"No," Hillsinger said. "Handwriting can be traced."

Billy stood up again, left the room, and returned with a type-writer and a stack of paper. He typed out a full page of names and addresses next to dollar amounts. There were twenty-two entries in all.

"I'm impressed," Hillsinger said.

"All of it was in cash. If anyone asks, I'll deny everything."

Hillsinger looked at the list.

"These names are obviously aliases," Hillsinger said, "but I should warn you that if even one of these entries is completely fictitious—i.e., if you are just making people up—I will know that, and our deal will be off. Also, if you alert Kallenbach to having given me this information, I will know that, too, and our deal will be off."

"Understood," Billy said.

Hillsinger left through the kitchen door and Wilkie followed, apologetically. Billy put the cast-iron pan in the oven for a few minutes to finish the steak. He was left with the clear impression that Jim Hillsinger had just traded his wife to him for a list of names.

87

The Old Man's funeral was the next day. The family walked out the back door in a loose procession to the graveyard, which lay between the back pasture and the woods. At the top of the hill, Catta stood just behind a half-circle of people in the bright sun around a hole dug in the midst of the other headstones. The names on the stones were familiar: Hillsingers and Quicks and the minor offshoots. It was the kind of day his grandfather had loved, the sun was hot and the wind cool. Those days, he had said, confuse the body but clarify the mind. This gathering, these surroundings, even the idea of a service—it was all ridiculous when measured against his grandfather's outsized rage and jubilation, the sheer force of his presence. That pine box could never hold the Old Man for five seconds, let alone for eternity.

Look, Catta, his mother had said to him that morning when he walked into the Hill House, scrubbed, brushed, wearing a borrowed tie. His mother's hair was all pulled back, and she wore a black dress with an exploding white flower pinned to her chest.

Cyrus found us peonies, she had said.

Next to the grave, Cyrus and his sons, Matthew and Mark, and Edward Peck lowered the pine box into the earth using long ropes. They each held one end, and the casket was balanced on the ropes between them as they let them out hand over hand in unison. The Episcopalian minister from Jennings read out the service. "In the sure and certain hope of resurrection," the minister said.

What do you know about it? Catta thought.

The day's perfection and maybe the silent procession up the hill, with his own father coming last, were the only parts of this that were worthy of the Old Man. They should have thrown him into the sea.

Billy Quick arrived late and stood next to Catta with his girls.

"What's in there?" Catta's little cousin Barbara whispered to Billy, pointing at the casket.

"That's Mr. Hillsinger," Billy said.

The long ropes at last went slack, and Cyrus and Edward Peck pulled them back up. The minister from Jennings invited anyone to step forward and throw a shovelful of earth on the box. His father did it, but no one else. Lila turned halfway round, smiled, and then bent down and whispered something to Isa, who walked back and took—not Catta's hand, as he was expecting— but the hand of little Barbara Quick, who stood next to him. Billy smiled, and the two girls stood there, at the edge of the circle, arms entwined, looking at the cows with their laughing bells.

88

At three o'clock the next afternoon, Catta stood on the edge of the dock, deciding whether to dive or not. Penny and George lay near him in the hot sun; they had been swimming already and were now drying slowly in the salt air. Five minutes earlier, Cyrus had left in the *Heron* for the mainland. He said the Migration had been a success—the lambs had made it safely to North Island.

Standing there, surveying the flat water of the harbor, Catta knew it would be cold. There would be, when he dove, the sharp intake of breath, the fierce embrace. He would swim out to the orange buoy and back and then climb up to lie on the dock next to the others, all three in a row with their heads on their hands. He would tell Penny and George the water was cold, which they already knew. All of that would happen soon enough. But for now, for this moment and perhaps for all the time still left to come, what he wanted most was to feel the sun's warmth on his bare skin.

Only that. Only the sun.

A Note on the Author

Estep Nagy's writing has appeared in *Southwest Review*, the *Believer*, the *Spectator*, *Paper*, and elsewhere. He is the writer and director of *The Broken Giant*, an independent feature film that is in the permanent collection of the Museum of Modern Art, and his plays have been produced across the United States as well as in the UK and Australia. He attended Yale University.